Best Tall Tales in Short Stories

Other Books by Winnfred Smith

Southern Shorts

Murder Finds a Home

Everybody Wants Madison

Best Tall Tales in Short Stories

Winnfred Smith

Winnfred Smith

LANIER
PRESS

LANIER PRESS *an Imprint of BookLogix*

Alpharetta, GA

ISBN: 978-1-61005-900-8

Library of Congress Control Number: 2017943259

10 9 8 7 6 5 4 3 2   0 7 1 9 1 7

Printed in the United States of America

∞This paper meets the requirements of ANSI/NISO Z39.48-1992 (Permanence of Paper)

Dedication

To my four mothers, who supported me with love and encouragement from the day I was born: Ruth (Rivers) Smith, my mother; Mattie Lola (Phillips) Rivers, my grandmother; Jane C. Rivers, my aunt; and Mattie Mae (Rivers) Loyd, my aunt.

Contents

Nonfiction

Acknowledgments

My appreciation goes to Lisa Folsom, Nicole Stuart, Gail Williams, and the Main Street Writers Association of Cartersville for critiquing these stories.

Fiction

Shining Knight

Todd asked himself a thousand times why he'd decided to go to the office today in the worst ice storm Sparta had seen in seven years. In a few hours, the temperature would drop to single digits. Now, with some car trouble on his way home, he found himself walking along a deserted road near dusk trying to maintain his footing on the ice-covered shoulder while questioning that ill-fated decision.

He knew the road well. It was six miles to the nearest house, but that wasn't a problem. He'd walked hours in heat and cold long ago. Today, he just had to keep concentrating on the hazardous surroundings, something he'd done before, in another life.

Up ahead he could see a familiar landmark, the old Carson Creek Bridge. It could withstand light traffic, but an eighteen-wheeler would send it crumbling into the creek some thirty feet below. *No matter,* he thought, *only the locals use it.* The four-lane over to the west took the heaviest loads now.

Todd was focusing so keenly on reaching the farmhouse he didn't notice how close he was to the shoulder's edge. He also didn't notice the sleet-covered tire tracks, now frozen, that led down the embankment. The cold, frozen ground cracked and broke under his boots. In an instant, he was sliding then tumbling till his feet stopped nearly touching the cold, raging waters, swelled by the rain of the last few days.

"You idiot," he said to himself.

There was no one to hear him, but it felt good. Todd picked himself up and began brushing the dirt and ice off his coat and pants.

A movement under the bridge caught his eye. A gloved hand went up. "Help me. Please help me," came the weak, female voice.

As he approached her, she made no movement. This young woman was lovely, almost angelic. Her golden hair glistening in the setting sunlight was just visible under the hood of her jacket.

"My name's Linda Sherman," she said. "Am I glad to see you. I've been here two hours. I thought I was going to die."

"I'm Todd. What happened?"

"My car slid off the road." She pointed to the old, light-green Volkswagen Beetle lying on its side. It was partially hidden by the tall bushes it had rolled over before coming to rest behind them. "I think I've broken my ankle. I tried to get up the bank, but it hurt real bad."

Todd gently touched her ankle. Linda winced a bit. He grimaced as he quickly offered his apologies, then added, "I don't think it's broken. More like a sprain. A sprain hurts worse than a break."

"Can't vouch for that, but this hurts a lot."

"You got anything else in the car?"

"Just my suitcase and makeup bag."

"We're going to leave those for now. Besides, you don't need any makeup," he said without thinking. It just slipped out. Linda tossed him a sweet smile. He found her very beautiful, though she seemed so frail lying there in pain. "We'll come back for them."

"Okay. I'm sure glad you came along."

"We'll see. First I have to get you up the bank."

It was not his strength he questioned, but his ability. Todd knew the ice would be a formidable obstacle he had to overcome.

"Sorry I'm so much trouble," said Linda.

"You're no trouble. I'm gonna bend down. I want you to climb onto my back. I'll need both hands and feet to work the bank. Now climb on," he said, bending down and digging in with all fours.

Linda did as he asked, wrapping both her slender arms around his neck.

About halfway up one foot slipped. His hands dug through the snow and he held on to the grass underneath, but he went flat, to the ground, with Linda dropping on top of him.

She uttered a sudden but calm, "Aii," expressing her discomfort.

"Sorry. Hold on."

Todd lifted himself and his load again, struggling for every inch of earth to grasp hold of. She seemed light as a feather. This time he made it to the top. He dropped to his knees and Linda slid off his back, rolling to the ground.

She lay there staring at the darkening sky, then whispered, "You did it. You're wonderful. Thank you."

"It's been a long time."

Linda sat up, leaning back on her hands. "What was that?"

He rolled over onto his back. "Oh, nothing. Just thinking out loud. We better get up before the dampness soaks through."

Todd positioned himself for her to mount his back. "Climb on."

"You don't have to do this, you know."

"If I don't, you'll have to hop for the next six miles."

"Gotcha," said Linda, looking up at him with a smile.

She climbed on his back, again folding her arms snugly around his neck. Todd raised himself to his feet and began their journey. Linda swung her legs forward so Todd could catch them in his hands. Her head lay resting on her arms but also against his head.

"What were you doing out here?" asked Todd.

"Going to visit my parents. They live nearby. I kept taking detours because of the storm, but managed to find my way here. I nearly slipped off several times, but this last time I lost it. I thought I was going to die, when you saw my car and came to my rescue."

"I didn't see your car. Doubt anyone would have."

"Doesn't matter. You found me. You're my knight in shining armor."

"I'm no knight. Besides, we still have to get to the house and a phone. Mine's broke. Do you have one?" asked Todd.

"No, but I'm not worried," she said sweetly and tightened her arms for a moment to emphasize her meaning.

Todd liked that little squeeze she gave him. It had been a long time since he had felt that. How many times had he carried someone, on his back just like this, out of some building? But those days were over. *How ironic*, he thought. He found someone he wasn't looking for and now he was carrying her, on his back, in the freezing cold, rescuing her—and himself.

"Tell me about yourself?" he asked.

"Well, I'm twenty-three, from Chattanooga, lived there most of my life but born here in Riverwood. Mom's not feeling well, so I'm going to stay with them for a few weeks. It will be great to see my parents again. I really miss them."

"Sounds like you love them a lot."

"Yes I do. They worked hard to help me through college. They were always there when I needed them. Mom's a great mom and great cook. Makes the very best coffee. And my dad, well, he's really special," said Linda.

"I'm puzzled. Why didn't you just take the four-lane?"

"What four-lane? I didn't know there was a four-lane," she said.

"It's been there several years."

"Oh . . . well, I always use this one," said Linda. "What kind of work do you do, Todd?"

"Computers."

"Computers seem so exciting. I don't know a thing about them."

"They're not exciting at all."

"You seemed to know what you're doing, rescuing and all, and you're very strong," she said as she squeezed his arm. "Have you ever rescued anyone?"

Todd thought for a moment on how to answer that question. Just the thoughts were painful. He couldn't remember the last time he'd spoken of them, but figured he need not lie. "Yes, years ago."

"Tell me about it. I want to hear," she said.

"I'd rather not."

"It must have been a bad experience. Please tell me? It sometimes helps, to talk about it, I mean. I'm a good listener," she said.

Those memories had been well hidden for years, kept under emotional lock and key. Now, she wanted him to open the lid again. So what, he'd done it before.

"I was a fireman—once."

"Then you *have* rescued people?"

"Many times."

"But something happened? I want to know. Please?"

"We were called to a three-story apartment building, an old one. It was burning bad when we got there, and we were looking for anyone left inside. I opened a door on the third floor and found a family of nine, but the two adults were dead. Smoke, I figured. I carried two of the children to the stairs and transferred them to Billy, my partner, but that was it. The stairs were now in flames, so I called for a ladder."

"Todd, that was so awful. What did you do?"

"I wrapped the two youngest in wet towels. They were all unconscious, but I moved them next to the window, when the place started falling apart. The whole room filled with burning beams from the floors above. One hit me in the chest, pushed me against the dresser. An oil lamp fell off and busted on the floor right next to the three older kids. The oil ignited all around them, their clothes . . ." Todd stopped.

He felt drops of water on his neck. They had to be from Linda's eyes.

"I've never heard anything like that before. If you don't want to go on . . . it's okay."

Todd had started the story; he could finish it. The "shrinks" made him tell it often.

"I grabbed a blanket to smother the flames. One of the girls came to and started screaming and running around the room. I continued to snuff the flames of the other two. She was terrified, wouldn't listen. She ran out the room and fell into the burning stairwell.

"Frank and Phil came up the ladder. Each took one of the older kids. I had the two younger ones in my arms, when the floor gave way under us. The whole building was coming apart. I fell two floors still holding the two children. One child died. I lived."

Those drops of tears were now streaming down from Linda's eyes to his neck. "My dear Todd." Her voice cracked, her arms gripped him tighter. "You quit being a fireman after that, didn't you?"

"Yes. Couldn't even suit up. The 'shrinks' told me it would pass, but it didn't. I went to night school. Now I'm in the IT field."

Linda gave him another hug. "I'm sorry the child died, but I'm glad you didn't." The tenderness in her voice was almost forgiving. "If you had died, you wouldn't be here saving me." Todd was still quiet. Linda continued. "You know, Todd, some say we all have a destiny."

"And mine was to rescue you, huh?"

"Yes."

"I didn't know you needed saving. I had to slip down a bank to see you."

"What would have happened to me if you hadn't come along?"

"With the temperature dropping, you would have frozen to death."

"You saved my life. And see, there's the farmhouse up ahead."

He hadn't even noticed it, but then he hadn't walked six miles either.

"I don't understand."

He stumbled and fell to the ground. Linda fell with him and rolled to the side, then stood up.

When Todd looked at her she was more beautiful than he remembered. A smile covered her face.

"Sorry. I tripped on something. You all right?" he asked.

"Yes, I'm fine, but I must go now," she said.

"I got news for you. You can't go anywhere without me. But no. You're standing. Your foot?"

"Todd, you're a wonderful, kind man who has lost faith in himself, but I forgive you for that. A princess may forgive her knight. And Todd, you have nothing to be ashamed of or sorry for."

"What're you talking about?"

"You, Todd. I'm talking about a strong man who has risked his life for others and now me. We are eternally grateful. I will always remember you."

"Wha . . ." was all Todd could say when Linda faded away, smiling, the most beautiful . . .

Todd felt disoriented. He got to his feet and looked around. He was alone. He looked down where Linda had lain. The ice was undisturbed. Looking back down the road, he saw no footprints. The icy road was completely smooth, and for the first time since he'd met her, he was very cold.

The farmhouse was dimly lit but warm. Todd called for a wrecker while the old woman made him coffee.

"Coffee's great. I'm Todd Billings. You've been very kind."

"You're welcome," she said. "I'm Elsa Sherman." Her voice cracked with the sounds of age.

Todd's eyes lit up. This couldn't be. "If you don't mind, do you live alone?"

"Why, yes, young man, I do. My husband's been dead since sixty-six, right after our daughter died."

Could this be a coincidence? "Would you mind telling me your daughter's name?"

"Linda. Her name was Linda."

"Please tell me what happened to her."

"Well, young man, it was winter and she was coming to see me in January of nineteen and sixty-six when her car slid off the road, at the Carson Creek Bridge. You must have crossed it tonight."

"Yes. Please continue."

"She managed to get out of the car, but the sheriff said she couldn't climb the bank. She'd injured her foot. The temperature dropped to near zero that night. She froze to death there under the bridge. Oh, my . . ." The old woman paused for a moment. "If only someone could have seen her car."

"There're lots of bushes, and after dark, no one would have seen it."

"Why, that's just what the sheriff said, but how did you know?"

"Just . . . just a guess. You said your husband also died in nineteen sixty-six."

"He always felt he could have saved her. She was so close to home, so close to him. But there was nothing he could do. I tried to tell him. Yet, he blamed himself for her death. He couldn't live with it."

"There was nothing he could have done. He shouldn't have blamed himself."

"You're very kind to say."

Thoughts of his fireman days intervened. "Sometimes we blame ourselves for things we have no control over. No control whatsoever. We think and we hope we could have done more . . ." Todd trailed off, lapsing into himself for a moment. "If anyone had seen her, I'm sure they would have saved her. I wish I could have."

"Linda would have liked you," said the old woman.

"Ma'am?"

"You have an understanding heart. She'd see that right off, and you've not used one cuss word. She didn't take to men who cussed. She was always looking for her knight—"

"Her knight in shining armor," Todd finished without thinking.

"Yes. Yes. That's what she always said. I only wish . . ." She didn't finish the sentence but turned to get the coffeepot to freshen Todd's cup.

"Do you have a picture of Linda?"

"I have one on the mantel. It's always there. I'll show you."

They walked to the living room. The old woman pointed to the picture on the mantel framed by two small, white candles.

It was Linda. Her blond hair was as brilliant as it had been today. The small body, the unmistakable smile. It was her—standing beside a light-green Volkswagen.

Todd was beginning to understand. Linda had needed rescuing, but there had been no one there to do it. She was worth saving and should have been saved. Now he understood. You can't save everyone, but you save those you can. He then realized Linda had saved him. And something or someone had let him save her, if only for a moment in some other time.

THE END Worth Saving

He and the Freezing She

He had been many a place but never here. Usually it was very hot or very cold. But this was different. They had hidden her here. The question was, where was here? How could anything live with snow three feet deep sitting on top of unknown feet of ice? It didn't matter. They said she was here, and here was where he would begin his search.

It was a long night and dawn had shown its cold, menacing face. The boss was surprised when he had asked for a dog-sled team. But this was not the first time he had needed one.

In a prior time, he had had to find a man and his daughter. The daughter he had found alive, but the man had provided her with clothing and cover to keep her warm. His actions had saved his daughter. The man had been found frozen to the point of cracking like a block of ice.

A few miles to the colder north was now where he had to go.

His five-foot-eleven height offered some advantage to manning the sled, but the dogs knew the routine. From the details he was given, she was five six and about 105 pounds. Easily transportable.

If his plans worked out, he would not lose this "she." His management team was lucky to have found her. He was told she was twenty-three with blond streaks in her brown hair.

But he wondered why she was in this frozen, desolate place.

All she did was witness a robbery and give her story to the police. An innocent human trying to do the right thing, not knowing the depth of what she had seen. The group or mob or gang of evil by whatever name that had planned the theft had decided to make an example of her. She was to simply die and never be found.

But someone had talked and disclosed her general location. And he was now here looking for she.

Now miles north and snowing, a break would be appreciated but not expected. He continued for another two miles or more.

A cave just in sight drew his attention, and he let himself believe it was the right one. He began raking snow aside with his bare hands to clear the opening.

There she was, bundled and shivering. It was she.

"Are you okay?" he asked.

"What do you expect in this godforsaken place? What took you so long?" she demanded.

"You left a poor trail. Come to think of it, I left my coffee back at camp. Be back in a few hours. Keep comfortable."

With that, he turned and started walking to the cave entrance. With his back to her, he smiled, wishing he could see her face.

Just as he was at the cave entrance, she let out a scream.

He swung about to face her. "Did you say something?"

She was not happy. Growling, she said, "Just where do you think you're going? You're supposed to rescue me!"

"No. I was to rescue a nice, sweet, appreciative woman, happy to see the guy who came over five miles in three feet of icy snow. But it seems you are not the right rescue."

With that said, he stood there to see what she would do.

She became quiet, and he wondered what she was thinking. Her eyes began to water.

Very quietly she began, "I'm sorry. Please forgive me. I've been so cold and scared I just couldn't think clearly. I said my prayers. I was going to die, then you appeared. Please forgive me. I'm so very sorry."

"Ah, good. I thought I had the right woman."

With that, he gave her water and more clothing. Heavy clothing. He had brought a spare set of boots. She needed them; hers were ripped and leaking. He removed her ragged boots, dried her feet with a towel, then held them against his chest for a bit to warm them. When they felt warm, he put fresh socks and boots on her small, pretty feet.

Tears were running down her cheeks. He gave her a piece of cloth to wipe her tears. She looked at him and offered a silent thank-you with her lips. He smiled in return.

They walked to the cave opening, where he picked her up and placed her snugly in the dog sled before tying her in. He placed a kiss on her forehead. Her eyes were now dry and had a happy, peaceful glow. She pulled him back close and whispered in his ear.

He brought her back to civilization safe and unharmed. He delivered her to her home in Riverside. It was a peaceful, warm, Southern town, as he had found they all were. His boss gave him two weeks off, and he spent it in Riverside fulfilling the whispered wish she had asked of him.

THE END, with a Thankful She

Mall Mice

"She must be on her way," said Samantha, phone still in hand. "No one's at home." Samantha's mother was usually good about picking them up.

"What about your dad? Shouldn't he be there?" asked Wanda.

Samantha was still listening to the ringing.

"No, he's away on a business trip. Remember, I told you. Don't you remember anything?" Samantha left a message and hung up the phone.

Wanda and Samantha came to Midtown Mall every Saturday, where they spent the day window-shopping and visiting with friends while never spending more than a few dollars. Wanda's parents were away on an extended weekend, so she was staying at Samantha's, something they both had been looking forward to. A perfect weekend for a couple of thirteen-year-olds.

"It'll be okay. She's just a little late," said Wanda.

Wanda's mother never showed up on time. Being picked up late was normal for her.

It was now almost an hour past closing. Everyone was gone, even Billy. The mall closed at ten, but it took another half hour or so for all the clerks in the stores to close up and go home. It always took that for Mr. Randall and Billy, his helper, to straighten up the Pizza Parlor. Samantha liked to talk and watch Billy close up, so Samantha's mom collected her around ten thirty, just about the time Billy left.

Samantha's mother was sometimes a little late. But tonight, Samantha's mother was very late.

"Hi. You girls okay?" Samantha and Wanda jumped. "You two got a way home?" asked the security guard. His voice boomed and echoed from the end of the empty hall.

"Yes, sir. My mother. She's a little late, but she's on her way," said Samantha, sounding more confident than she felt.

"Well, let me know if you need something. Wait inside, not outside, okay?"

"Thanks, Mister. We will," said Samantha.

The guard continued his rounds and disappeared behind one of those Employees Only doors. The parking lot was empty. It was ten forty-five and very quiet.

"Wonder if the guard thinks we're mall rats? The older boys do. He probably does, too. Do you think?" asked Wanda.

Samantha was so intent on finding her mother out there, somewhere, that Wanda's words took a moment to register. She turned to answer her.

"What? No, I don't think so. He's nice." Then looking back through the glass, she said to herself in almost a whisper, "Mama, where are you?"

"What?" asked Wanda.

"Oh, nothing. Nothing."

"Oh. Okay. You know, I don't like the term 'rats' anyway," continued Wanda. "If anything, we're mall mice. We're not old enough to be rats. And it sounds a lot better."

That drew Samantha's full attention.

"No, it doesn't. And I'm no mouse, big or small, and neither are you. You know what happened to Jaime Ferguson when he called me a mall rat?"

Wanda grinned. "Yeah, you kicked him in the ... you know."

"And I'd do it again."

Wanda stared at the darkness outside and the cavernous halls behind her. This frightened her, and when she got frightened, she started talking.

"Samantha, you ever wonder why we're friends?"

Samantha was startled by the question. "Not really. We just are. Why?"

"I don't know. I was just thinking, and well, you're so smart. You're smarter than any of the boys we know. Everybody likes you. And you're prettier than I am, and . . ." Wanda paused. Samantha started to interrupt, but decided not to.

Wanda continued. "And I bug you sometimes, like now, when I talk too much. I mean, I know why you're my best friend. You help me with my homework. You make me feel better when I don't feel good. You listen to me. You talk to me. And you take care of me. But I don't know why you want me as a friend."

Something was happening that didn't happen often: tears were forming in Wanda's eyes.

"Wanda, that's a pretty deep thought. First of all, stop putting yourself down. I'm not prettier than you are. We're just pretty in different ways. And I'd never pass a math test if it weren't for you. And yeah, you do need a little taking care of. You're a little naïve, and I envy you for that."

"Really?" asked Wanda.

"Really. I figure I'll grow up and have a bunch of babies, and you'll be a scientist. Somebody important."

"Really?" Wanda asked again.

"Yes, and stop saying *really* or I'll take you off my best-friend list. And, seeing as you are the only one on the list, well, it would be a little lonely."

Samantha spread her arms. Wanda stepped into them and they hugged. After a few moments, they separated. Both now had tissues to dab their eyes.

"Well, guess I better try Mom again," said Samantha as she pulled out her phone, but the battery was dead. She slid it into the back pocket of her jeans. She found a pay phone, the only one in the mall, and used her last quarter to try her mother again. No answer.

"Something's wrong. It only takes Mom twenty minutes, max, to get here. She should be here by now."

She meant to hang up before the answering machine picked up, but didn't make it. The pay phone kept her quarter.

"I gotta go to the bathroom," said Wanda.

"You always have to pee. Go on. I'll wait here."

"No way," said Wanda. "This place is spooky. Please, come with me. I gotta go real bad."

Samantha gave in.

"Wanda, what's keeping you?" asked Samantha while she combed her silky hair, something she still liked her mom to do.

"I had a little problem, but it's fine now. Be out in a minute."

Samantha checked her watch. Almost eleven.

Wanda emerged from the stall. She washed and dried her hands, then primped her long, dark hair. "Okay. Let's go."

They headed back to the entrance.

The mall was dim now. Many of the lights had been turned off. The neon lights that made the mall festive while open now cast eerie glows, and dark shadows scaled the walls.

Just as they made the turn toward the doors, they heard a noise at the far end of the mall.

"Did—did you hear that?" asked Wanda, startled, as her hands went to her lips.

"Yes." Samantha pointed toward the department store. "It came from down there."

"I'm scared," said Wanda.

"Don't worry. It's just the security guard. They hang around all night."

"How do you know that?"

"Billy told me. We'll probably see him again. I'm going to make another phone call."

"You going to try your mother again?"

"No, I'll call Lisa. Her mother will pick us up. I used my last quarter. Give me your phone."

"I don't have it. I left it at home for Mama to use. But I got a quarter," said Wanda, nodding and bouncing on her tiptoes.

Samantha called Lisa, but Lisa's mother and father were still out. Lisa's brother, Mark, would come get them. They were to wait at the main entrance.

"I'm so glad Lisa was home. At least someone knows we need them," said Wanda.

"Yeah. I feel better now."

Another noise broke the silence. Wanda stared silently, mouth open, at Samantha.

"Yeah, I heard it too. It's just the guard making his rounds. He has to open and shut doors, doesn't he?" But Samantha knew it didn't sound like a door.

Wanda was afraid and tried to open the outside door. It was locked. "The door's locked. I thought the doors were always open."

"The guard must have locked them while we were in the restroom. He probably thought we left. Come on, let's go find him. We have about twenty minutes before Lisa and Mark get here."

They walked out into the mall. Samantha gave a forceful "HELLO! Anyone here? We need help!" Silence. Samantha said again, louder, "HELLO? Where are you, Mister? We heard you! We need to get out of the mall. We've got someone picking us up. OKAY?" More silence.

But Samantha had an answer. "Come on. He went into that employee entrance. That's why he can't hear us."

The girls found the hallway the guard had entered earlier and opened the door. The hall was lit, but dim and long. As they walked, they passed mailboxes and office doors, until they finally came to one marked "Mall Security."

"I bet he's in here," said Samantha.

They opened the door. Through the dim light they could see someone seated behind a desk in the corner. After a couple of "hellos" and "hey Misters" with no answer, Samantha moved toward the desk. Samantha was about halfway, when Wanda, still near the door, found and flipped the light switch.

Samantha uttered a small gasp, startled by the sudden brightness. As her eyes focused, she saw the security guard, with a small stream of blood on the left side of his chest. His head was leaning back, exposing his thin neck and his bulging Adam's apple. His arms hung limp beside the chair. Wanda moved beside Samantha.

"Is . . . is he dead?" asked Wanda.

"Like, how am I supposed to know? I'm thirteen. A kid. I may watch NCIS, but I'm not a medical examiner," she exclaimed, frustrated.

"Oh, my dad loves NCIS. Watches it all the time. I do too."

"Not now, Wanda. Look at him."

"He looks dead!"

"Yeah . . . he does."

Samantha walked around the desk and gave the guard a gentle nudge. He rocked, fell sideways, and bounced off the desk to the floor.

Samantha screamed. Then Wanda. They ran from the room crying, down the hall, and didn't stop till they reached the mall entrance. The doors were still locked. They turned and leaned back against them. The only sound was their crying, and finally only their sniffling, as they wiped the tears from their eyes.

"What're we going to do?" asked Wanda, becoming quiet.

"I don't know," Samantha said, suddenly timid.

They heard a door open and slam shut.

"Oh, God. Did you hear that?" asked Wanda.

"Yes, and it's *not* the guard." Samantha regained her composure.

"Then it must be . . ."

Samantha finished the sentence. "The murderer. And he knows we're here."

They clutched each other tightly.

"I hear his footsteps," said Samantha. "Keep quiet. Get down behind the wastebin. He knows we're here, but he may not know where."

Both girls huddled behind the wooden waste container that rested about halfway down the short hall leading out the main entrance. The footsteps stopped. Samantha took a quick peek around the waste container to see the killer looking down the wide hallway, now dim.

Turning back, she looked at Wanda. Before she could speak, they heard him come nearer then stop. After a thousand long seconds, they heard him walking farther away till his footsteps were silent.

"Now what do we do?" whispered Wanda.

"We're going to throw the trash can through that door."

"What?"

"They do it in movies all the time. We'll break the glass with the trash can and we'll be outside—and safe."

Samantha guided Wanda. They lifted the wooden frame covering the trash can and set it quietly down to the side. The trash can was metal, not too heavy by itself, but the trash inside gave it some weight. They struggled to lift it then ran toward to door, stopped short, and threw it with all their might at the glass, but part of the can caught the crossbar, allowing only the top to strike. It made a lot of noise.

"Criminy," said Samantha as she looked at the unbroken glass, the trash strewn over the floor, and their wasted effort. "He'll be back now. We gotta get out of this dead end."

When they got to the main hallway, the sheer size of the walkways brought fear. They grabbed each other's hand. But they stopped. They saw a dark figure at the far end turn a corner and start walking fast toward them.

"Run!" shouted Samantha. "Run!"

They ran toward the department store and shook the large chain gate. It wouldn't move. They turned and looked at the doors to the employee entrance.

"I don't want to go back there," said Wanda.

"We have no choice. Follow me."

Crying, Wanda followed Samantha, who grabbed the door and threw it open. It slammed hard against the wall. Samantha started trying all the doors they had passed only a few minutes ago. They were all locked except the one the guard was in. They passed it and stopped where another hall crossed.

"Which way, Samantha? Which way do we go? We're going to die, aren't we?"

Samantha's mind was running a hundred miles an hour. Think. Daddy always said she could get anything she wanted from him. She just had to put her mind to it.

"One of these doors has to lead outside."

"Maybe they just lead to other stores," said Wanda, close to crying.

"No. Remember, we passed some mailboxes back there." Wanda nodded.

"Well, we never see a mailman in the mall, because they must have their own entrance. Come on. Follow me." Samantha knew they had to keep moving. This might be the way out.

Both girls ran with all their strength, and when they came to the door, they threw themselves against it then fell back to the floor. The door didn't budge. Samantha got up and pressed the handle over and over, but the door wouldn't open.

"Now what, Samantha?"

"Hm. They might all be locked. Wanda, you still have that can of mace in your pocketbook?"

"Yeah. Why?"

"Just hold on to it."

Samantha grabbed Wanda. They turned around and headed back to where the halls crossed. "Come on." Up ahead she could see an oversized manhole cover. "Help me," she said as she bent over and grabbed it.

The cover was heavy, but the girls slid it to one side far enough for them to slip past it. Samantha had a small pocket flashlight on her key chain. With it she could see a ladder leading down about eight feet into what looked like a tunnel. A tunnel full of pipes and cables.

"Let's go," said Samantha.

"Down there? I do *not* want to go down there."

"Then stay up here and die."

Samantha knew Wanda would follow. Samantha skimmed past the cover onto the ladder. Wanda followed. Together they pulled the cover back into place, just as the murderer opened the outer door. The cover closed with a *clink*.

Samantha and Wanda quietly moved down the ladder to the damp, dirt floor below and moved back against the wall.

Samantha wanted to hold her mother so much right now. *Oh, Daddy, Mama*, she thought. *I love you so much.* What if her mother was dead, and then she died here? Her daddy would be alone. Samantha prayed, *If I have to die, let Mama live.* But Samantha was not ready to give up. Not yet.

She took the can of mace from Wanda's pocketbook.

"Now, be very quiet," whispered Samantha as she held the light on the floor in front of them.

"Oh, God," Wanda whispered. "What's that?" She pointed to something the size of a cat.

"It's a rat. A very big rat. I *hate* rats. Oh, God. I really hate rats." Now even Samantha was scared.

Just then the cover flew off and light poured into the cavern. The girls muffled a scream with their hands. They stood paralyzed.

"Well, girls, looks like I found you," said the killer as he made his way down the ladder, gun drawn.

He stepped onto the floor and turned to face the girls.

As he did, Samantha filled his face with the flashlight and a second later filled it full of mace.

"What the—" said the killer as he stepped back, rubbing his eyes, his face burning. But it wasn't over. He stumbled backward and stepped on the rat, who then took a plug out of his leg. He screamed in pain and fell, landing on the rat, who took another bite. The killer's head crashed against the pipes.

He lay still.

"Is he dead?" asked Wanda.

"I don't care. We're getting out of here," said Samantha.

They scrambled up the ladder and slid the cover back over the hole.

Just then a door opened and several flashlights appeared. The girls were ready to run the other way when they heard the two most beautiful words.

"Stop! Police!"

They stopped. Samantha turned. "Boy are we glad to see you guys. The killer's down there."

She and Wanda pointed to the manhole cover.

A policeman approached the girls. "Killer? What killer?"

"The one who shot the guard and chased us down that manhole," said Samantha, pointing again. "He's down there."

They explained all that had happened.

"But how did you know we were here?" asked Samantha.

He explained that someone had set off a silent alarm, and as they were checking all the doors, the police had heard someone trying to get out the side door. That turned out to be the one the girls had tried.

When Samantha told the police about the trash can, they found the security tape circling the window had been broken just enough to send another alarm.

When asked why they didn't use the phone in the security office, Samantha said she didn't think of it.

"Well, I did," said Wanda. "But there was a dead man in there and I wasn't going near it."

Their story made the local newspaper and depicted Samantha and Wanda as the heroines they were. The killer had escaped from the local prison and was hiding in the mall planning to steal whatever he could and leave the next day. Samantha was pleased with how the journalist told the story—how they had captured the killer and how her mother had been in an accident and would recover.

Their mall hours were cut back. That gave Billy more reason to pay extra special attention to Samantha.

Everything worked out great except one thing. When Samantha saw the title, on the front page, she knew who was responsible.

It read, "Mall Rat Saves Mall Mice."

THE END

Clanton's Store

"Morning, young lady," I said as I ambled through the glass-paned door, which had replaced the wooden door I once pranced and skipped through forty-five years earlier.

She was setting in a wicker chair just inside the front door.

"Hello, Mister. If you see anything you like, let me know. We're selling everything. Everything that's left, that is," said the pert, twenty-three-year-old woman, her voice littered with rising intonations.

I looked around the old store, once a thriving business, as thriving as a small-town center store in the humid flatlands of southern Louisiana could be. Now, only the fixtures remained.

I moved around the store, thinking of past visits, and my drooling over chocolate kisses, as I called them. And the all-day suckers and Tom cookies. So many memories.

Those were the days. The days I lived with my parents in a small, three-room house where I walked from up the road to Clanton's Store to buy as much candy and cookies as my nickels and pennies would allow.

The young, chestnut-haired woman was reading a book. "Whatcha reading?" I asked.

"Oh, it's just an old novel, *The Body in the Library*, by Agatha Christie. It's about—"

I jumped in. "A young woman was found dead in the library of an English country home. It's a Miss Marple tale, I believe."

"Yes, that's right. It is. Do you like Christie?"

"I thought everyone did." I smiled.

"I know I do." She returned the gesture.

"You know, you can't be his daughter. Too young. You must be a granddaughter. Clanton's grandchild. Right?"

"Yes, sir," she said, businesslike, then looked away— not wanting to talk more, it seemed.

"Did you know your granddad well?"

"No, sir. Not really. I mean, well, just let me know . . ."

"Don't want to talk about it, huh?"

"I'd rather not," she said shyly, head down, attempting to read as I continued prying.

I kept looking over the place. Clanton's. That was the name. It was long before Super Stops or Mini Markets. It could've had a sign: "Last chance to buy gas, fishing tackle, and candy for 50 miles." Well, not that far, but it was ten miles from the nearest small town, and in the fifties, that was a long way. There once were two stores. Eventually, Clanton had won out. Old man Clanton had died last year. The building and properties had been sold and now they were selling its contents.

It was early; the place was empty. From the back of the store I said, "Guess you didn't like him much?"

That startled her; she jerked a little. "I'm sorry, wha . . .? Oh, I—I just didn't know him very well. Mama didn't visit him much."

"I used to live here, you know. Just passing through today. I ought to introduce myself. I'm Bill Austin."

She sat up. "I'm Judy. Judy Taylor."

"Well, Judy Taylor, see that old black stove over in the corner?" I waved at it. "That stove was like a magnet that pulled many a man and boy in here. Made 'em feel at home. This was the kind of place where old men gathered to tell lies, lies about the biggest fish they caught and the women they loved. The younger men, well, they used to try and figure out who was lying the most."

She flashed a glimmer of a smile. "Yeah. I guess. Daddy mentioned that my granddad liked to fish a lot."

"That he did. Did they tell you what a good businessman your granddad was?"

"Yes, sir. That's all they ever talked about, really, was how much money he made. Mama was his youngest daughter. She moved away and went to school. They weren't very close."

"Yeah, your granddad was a good businessman. Old man Hartman had a store right beside this one. Did you know about him?"

"Mama didn't talk about it much, but Daddy always said how good a man Mr. Hartman was and how sad it was he had to sell out."

"I see. Then you know those two were in competition for many years. Old man Hartman sold his store, all right. Passed away soon after, as I remember. Your granddad bought it. Wasn't much of a place. Typical old country store: wood frame; tall, steep roof. Couldn'ta been more than fifteen feet square, but it made for good storage."

"That's too bad. I mean about the man dying and all." The knowledge was secondhand, but the compassion was first rate.

"Taylor. Yes. I remember now. You look just like your mother. Same hair. She wore it long, then, too. You got her eyes, too, you know, sort of golden brown. They sparkle just like hers. She was very beautiful, your mother. Married one of William Taylor's boys, right?"

She thanked me for saying so as she covered her mouth and nose with the book to hide her reddening face.

"Yes, sir. My father's name is Paul, and William Taylor is my other grandfather."

She stood up and walked over to where I was standing, by the old Coke machine.

The past became clearer.

"Tell me, what else did they tell you about your granddad Clanton?"

"Well," she paused for a moment, seeming reluctant to speak, "I probably shouldn't say, but you seem to know a lot about him and my family."

She lowered her head a little, then raised it.

"Daddy says that Granddad ran Mr. Hartman out of business and caused him to die. Is that what you heard? Is that why the man died? It's really hard to believe, you know. Granddad always sent me presents on my birthday, at Christmas, and many other times. He wrote me letters, but Mama didn't let me see them for a long time. I found him sweet and caring. But the others . . ." Her voice trailed off.

"Looks kinda slow right now. Why don't I tell you a story?"

The young woman nodded anxiously. She pulled the wicker chair she'd brought with her up near the old stove and sat down.

I found an old crate and did the same.

"You see," I started, "Hartman and your granddad were the best of friends since early childhood. They grew up out here together. Hartman was the older by about five years. That's a lot of difference when you're eleven and your best friend is sixteen. But there aren't many others to play with, so you had to pair up or play alone."

"I can see why they played together."

"Yep. Why, they hunted with makeshift spears made of cane poles, sharpened on the end, and made huts with tree limbs and pine needles. They went swimming in the Louisiana bayous, heading out in the morning and coming back in time for supper."

Judy jumped in. "I bet they had lots of fun!"

"Judy, they sure did. Oh, and they each had a dog. Boys had to have dogs, you know. It's written somewhere, at least, I suppose it is. They grew older and got married, Hartman first. Then they went off to war, Hartman first, again, to World War II, then your granddad to Korea."

"War is awful," Judy said quietly.

"Yes, it was. It is. But most had no choice. Now, while your granddad was in Korea, his friend bought the existing dry-goods store from someone whose name I forget and renamed it Hartman's General Store. It began to prosper, as did Brandon, the community building around it."

"I didn't know that. Mr. Hartman had a store first?"

"He did, and when your granddad returned from Korea, he continued raising his family, and with the help of a friend, built and opened Clanton's Store, right there next to Hartman's. Your granddad wasn't much of a farmer, but he did have a talent for selling things. He was good with people."

"This is so much I was never told."

"Well, there's even more to the story. Hartman wasn't upset at all, and being there first, was sure his business was safe. But your granddad's store began to build quickly and became a big success before either of them knew it. Judy, your granddad was not a greedy man, he just had a better way with people, and it paid off in customers. They both had gas pumps, but eventually Hartman stopped pumping gas and finally sold the store to your granddad."

Judy broke in while I was catching my breath.

"Mr. Austin, I didn't know about the rest, but that's how I heard it ended. You said Granddad wasn't greedy, but Mr. Hartman had to give up his business. If they were such good friends, why would Granddad open a store right next door to him? And why did he drive Mr. Hartman out of business?"

"There's a lot most people don't know, even your mama and your daddy. You see, Hartman talked him, your grandfather, into building the store. Remember, I said a friend loaned your granddad the money. It was Mr. Hartman. You see, Hartman didn't just stop selling gas and sell his store because business was bad. He was sick."

"Sick? What do you mean?"

"Mr. Hartman got cancer."

"No. Oh. Oh my. No one ever . . ."

"I know. No one ever knew. Those two kept it real quiet. In those days, wasn't much they could do for cancer. It had spread all over old man Hartman's body. He kept his doctor quiet. Wouldn't have been much they could have done, even today. He got so sick he couldn't run the pumps. As business dropped, so did his profits, but Hartman never let on to anyone except your granddad."

Tears were showing in Judy's eyes but I continued.

"Hartman was losing money, fast. Doctor bills were mounting, and he was about to lose his home. Your granddad offered to give him money, but Hartman wouldn't take it. Too proud. He had life insurance. That would take care of his family. But the only way Hartman could keep his home was to let the store go, so he made a secret deal with your granddad. A very well-kept secret. Almost like the kind of pledge two young boys would make to each other and sign in blood."

"But . . . if it was so secret, how did you know?"

I knew she'd ask. "I found out quite by accident. I went into Mr. Hartman's store one day while he was out front.

Guess he didn't see me going in. I was around on the far end of the candy counter, when he came in with your granddad. They were deep in a discussion and didn't see me. From what I started hearing, I decided to stay low and keep quiet. They stood near the front of the store and planned the whole thing, the selling of the store, I mean, and to keep it a secret. When they were through, they left, and I hightailed it outta there."

"Wow. They really cared about each other, didn't they?" Her tone had changed. Her words were warm.

I felt the question didn't need answering and I waited in silence.

"It's been so long," she said, sadly. Then, excited, she continued. "I should tell Mom and Dad and everyone. It's a wonderful story, and finally they'll know the truth about Granddad."

"No, you mustn't do that."

Her eyes flared. "But the stories about Granddad are false. He didn't do those things. He was a good man. He deserves better."

"He does, and I know how you feel. But your granddad cared more for his friend than what a few people thought they knew about him. I told you so you would know the truth. But you can't go passing this around. It would go against your granddad's wishes. You'd break his word. I know it's hard, but use what I've told you to love him and fight those who put him down."

Tears formed in her eyes. "Why did you tell me this? Now I know a secret I shouldn't know. A story I can't tell anyone. A story that would let everyone know that my grandfather was an honorable man. This is awful." Her hands covered her mouth.

"Maybe you're right. I probably shouldn't have. But when I saw what the stories did to your feelings for Mr. Clanton, well, you just had to know. I'm sure he loved you. You were his first granddaughter. I was once told that first granddaughters are always loved the most. And you must love him back. Even if no one else does, he has to have someone who cares. Some ancient civilizations believe the spirit can't rest unless it has someone among the living who loves it. And that someone is *you*. Reread those letters knowing what you know now."

She looked at me for every second of a minute, then wiped the tears from her eyes. I walked slowly to the front of the store, turned, and smiled.

"And you. You care, too?" she asked. Her voice broke.

"Yeah. And me."

"You sure kept up with everything, everyone."

"Just a little."

She looked at the car outside and saw a woman sitting in it. "That your wife?"

"Yes." I started walking to the front.

"You must have known my mother."

"For a short time, a long time ago."

"Oh," she said, puzzled. "Funny, she's never mentioned you."

"Well, we just knew each other briefly, then I left for greener pastures. I guess I should be going. Remember what

I told you. It was a pleasure to meet you. Your mother should be proud of you. You and your mother get along okay?"

"That's very kind of you to say, and yes, Mama and I are the best of friends," she said, still seeming unsure of me.

"I'm glad."

I turned and started toward the door. From behind me I heard a soft "Wait."

Judy walked to me, stood on her tiptoes, and with her small hands on my shoulders gave me a peck on the cheek.

"You're right. I'm glad I know. I'll remember everything. And I'll remember you, Bill Austin."

I continued to the door. My hand was on the knob, but before I could open it, from behind I heard:

"If you knew my mom before she got married, how did you know I was my granddad's first granddaughter? And you called him my granddad." Her words got softer. "That's what I called him. How did you know that?"

"I knew your mother before she was married. And I left after she got married. That's all. Brandon was a small town. Everyone knew everyone."

"Yeah, I guess so," she said.

"I have to go. Stay as sweet as you are."

With that, I put my hand on the door, pushed it open, and walked out. Behind me, in the open door, I heard her say, "Will I see you again?"

I turned to her and filled my heart one last time. I gave her a smile. It was not a question I wanted to answer.

We were about a mile down the road. Brandon grew smaller by the second. I hadn't said a word since I got in the car.

"You didn't tell her, did you?" said Laura, my wife, with a compassionate look from the passenger side.

"No. I didn't."

"But why? From the day you received the letter from her mother, you couldn't wait to see her. You went to great effort to find out when she would be here and finally got up the nerve."

"Laura, she's beautiful. I could hardly hold my joy just watching her and hearing her speak. She's smart. She's intelligent. She's intuitive, kind."

"You didn't answer my question."

I let out a breath of air. "My being a part of her life would only complicate it. If her mother had told me years ago I was her father, maybe. But not now. It's too late for me. Judy has a father. Her mother is a sweet woman. By sending the letter, she just wanted me to know the truth before she died. She isn't expecting anything. If she were, I'd have known long ago. Besides, if Judy knew her mother had an affair before she was born, it just might hurt their relationship, and I will not ruin their last year together."

"I knew I loved you for some reason."

I nodded and smiled. Staring ahead, I added, "But I did leave Judy a little something. I told her the Clanton-Hartman story."

"You didn't!"

"Yes. I did. Some of it may be flawed, but it contains a great deal of truth. Enough. She believed me, and that's what's important."

She shook her head. "They'll tell her it's not true. You know that."

"They'll try, but she won't believe them. The story will hold its weight. She loves her granddad now. No one's gonna take that away from her. For me, I don't know everything about her, but I know enough. I'll make it last a lifetime."

A Tender Never Ending

A 1942 Mystery
A Marlow Caper

Introduction

Before you start reading the story below, I want you to think Bogart. In case you don't know who that is, Humphrey Bogart was a movie star back in the forties. That's the 1940s, not the 1840s. They didn't do movies in the 1800s, but you may know that.

Now, if you ain't seen any Bogie movies—Oh, that was his nickname, Bogie. Okay, so if ya ain't seen any, go rent *Casablanca, Dead Reckoning,* or *To Have and Have Not.* Or try *The Maltese Falcon.* Okay, you get the point. Some of you ain't seen 'em, so we'll just take an intermission while you go rent one and watch it.

[Intermission in progress]

Okay, now you've got the gist of what Bogie sounds like. One of his most successful roles was Philip Marlowe, a detective. From there, Marlowe was played by five or six big-name actors up until the late fifties, as I recall.

Try to read the story below with Bogie's voice in your head. If you can't, it's okay. Just read the story and listen to your thoughts. Cheers.

Preface

Ever have one of those days when you wake up hoping the bright light illuminating the room is the moon? And having been warned by the alarm clock, you know you can't continue to deny reality: the sun's to blame.

I got a call from a woman named Lidia yesterday, Wednesday morning, and had a client chat with her. Business was slow and I figured why not. I needed the work and the moolah that attached itself. She's from Virginia. You're probably wondering why she, an out of towner, called me. So did I. Well, I *am* a private dick by trade. And I *am* in the yellow pages. Course, so are a dozen more gumshoes. Guess she flipped a coin.

Her brother is dead, the reason still unknown. The case ain't solved. And she's expecting *me* to solve it. The fee is worth contemplating the case. The woman, and there's always a woman in the game, is herself a mystery. Her name, as I said, is Lidia. Her brother's name was Thomas Mitchell. This is one of the most frustrating cases I've had in my career. Not difficult. Frustrating. I told my brain, "Marlow, get your brain in gear and get serious about this case." Oh, that's my name, Marlow. When we get to know each other better, we'll move to a first-name relationship.

I think it best I recap what I know. My brain needs confirmation. Thomas was killed in his apartment on Tuesday afternoon. Nothing was stolen—make that nothing notable was taken. Lidia suddenly arrived in town Wednesday morning—at least, that's what she told me—went to his apartment, and found him dead. That was obvious due to the bullet in his chest. Then she called me.

Did I mention there is another dame involved? And she ain't a relative, as far as I can tell. Her name's Katie Summer. She knew Lidia's brother. I confirmed that by *borrowing* a picture during my, shall we say, private visit to his apartment yesterday. The picture had words written on the back. Written by a woman. I could read the words—women write well. As to the picture, the police missed it, so I considered it mine.

Katie's a long-haired, foxy blond woman with blue eyes that I bet could put holes in your brain if you pissed her off. And no, I didn't figure that out from the picture. Well, maybe I did.

There was a phone number on the back, so I gave it a ring. It was a very short conversation. When you mention you're a private eye, everybody clams up. Anyway, I got enough to get a head start.

Miss Katie's a nightclub singer at the Charmers Club. I paid a visit, just to observe, you understand, last evening.

Wednesday, if you've forgotten. As I asked her questions, I thought we got along well.

Here's the story. Listen carefully, it could be interesting. I sometimes tell interesting stories.

The Story

Thursday came early, mostly due to the sun. I was pondering my actions and plans for the day regarding the case. My pondering was interrupted by mumblings a couple of inches away on the adjoining feather pillow. The double bed made it real cozy. A twin would have been too—make that very—cozy.

She mumbled as she snuggled closer to me. "Hi. Morning," she said softly, still half asleep with her pretty face half buried in the pillow. "You always up so early?"

I'd been laying on my back, observing the ceiling, and decided to roll to my right. It was a much better view. "It's after seven and the world awaits."

Her voice still soft and sleepy, she asked, "Was that a poem?" She snuggled even closer.

"Didn't intend it to be."

"Sounded like one," she yawned. "Do another," she said with a voice that a man, any man, would do anything to hear again.

"Katie's a cutie."

"Ooh, that was sweet."

Did I mention that her soft voice fit her physical components nicely?

"You're sweet, too, but I gotta get up. Got a case to work." I really did. And she was not helping.

She looked at me, her face sad. It was a beautiful face, regardless of expression, but she offered me more. She sat up in bed wearing what she had on when we got in bed last night. Nothing.

With no word uttered, she sat up on her knees with her legs spread, feet to each side. Her arms went up to straighten her long, blond hair. She then put those arms behind her, causing multiple points of interest to forcefully draw my attention.

"See anything of interest?" she asked.

Now, this was one of those times when us guys can win or feel the concrete block dragging us under. And it would be the deepest hole any ocean had to offer.

So I gave it a try. "See," I pointed to my eyes, "I had to close 'em. You're melting my brain along with my will. Please, lay back down here. Please?"

I opened one eye to see a devilish smile on her face. She snuggled down beside me. Okay, so I got lucky. Trick was, how long would it last? I opened both eyes.

She turned her head to the side a wee bit. "You still *really* want to get up, don't you?"

"If I say yes, what will happen?"

"I'll show you later. We can get up. I'll fix you some breakfast and melt your brain later. Hope you have some milk in the icebox." She kissed me and crawled off the bed with movements that were indescribable. I followed with what little mind I had left.

We dressed and she fixed breakfast.

We were sitting at my would-be kitchen table. She was eating with slow, small bites, as I imagined a woman would. I was scooping and gorging myself. Katie was watching me with an understanding look. The conversation was only about pleasant things, mostly her and the food. But I needed some *unpleasant* things cleared up.

Slowing my gorging and turning from my food, I figured it was the moment. "We've talked about a lot of nice things, but I really need to know something."

"Okay, sure. What is it?" Her response was cheerful and understanding. It made me want to leave town because I figured this would change the mood.

"You told me last night that Thomas Mitchell did something for you, but you wouldn't say what. I really do need to know." I waited for an answer or a reaction. I hoped both would be pleasant.

"I don't like you doing your detective thing." She didn't like the subject change, that was obvious. But why?

"A man's dead and I have a client wanting to know why. I have to. No choice."

"I know, Sam. Please understand how I know, I mean knew, Tommy. He was a special guy. Only trying to help."

"Did you two have a, ah, relationship?"

"Damn you. I know what you're thinking." She teared up as she spoke. I didn't know why, but somehow I was to blame. Still, I'm a man, so what'd you expect?

Grabbing a fresh napkin—I was out of tissues—I moved around to her chair and got down on my knees.

Handing her the napkin, which she accepted, I said, "Yes, I was thinking that, and I think my thought was off base. But understand, the words on the back of the picture were personal. 'Love ya' caught my attention."

She looked down at me while dabbing at her remaining tears. "We spent a lot of time together. We went places together. We were close." She stopped dabbing, paused, and added, "Tommy was my brother."

That was sudden news. "Your brother?" *Now she tells me.*

"I'm sorry. I was afraid to tell anyone after what happened."

"What was that?"

"This is an awful thing to say. Oh, I don't like this." She shook her head as if trying to force the words out. "Okay. Here goes. The owners of the club wanted me to be extra nice to some of their customers. Special customers. I know you know what they wanted me to do. Sam, that's not me. I'm no call girl. I said no and made the mistake of telling Tommy. Now he's dead and I caused it."

That was all it took. She was now in a full crying spell. She pushed her chair back and dropped to the floor, holding on to me as if the floor would open up and swallow her.

"He obviously cared about you. Katie, he was doing what us guys do for our girls. Protect. But we don't know if you're the cause." That didn't slow her tears. I slowly pulled back and took her soft face in my hands. "Now, you listen. I need *your* strength and help. I now have *two* problems to work out."

With tears slowing and tissue wet, she said, "I'll leave and one of your problems will be gone. I'm trouble for everyone." Her head shook again from side to side. Her hands dropped to her lap.

"Baby, you ain't no problem. If you *were* a problem, you'd be the kind us men want to hang on to." She looked at me. No expression. I shook her head gently, and she made a small, feminine noise. Her hands grasped my arms. "Forgive me, but I need your attention. I really do need your help, okay?"

"Yes. I'll help." She still sounded shaky. "That's good. I'm glad to know you're Tommy's sister. Did you two have any siblings? More brothers or sisters?"

She seemed to smile, her face peaceful. "I like you. I really like you." She paused a moment, just looking at me. Then she shook her head and her eyes came to attention, like she suddenly woke up. "Huh? Oh. No. Just us two. Parents dead. We're it. Why are you asking?"

My hands found hers. "You were a surprise. I don't need any more."

She was perking up more. "I don't want you to get any more surprises."

"You were—you are—one nice surprise. Why did you spend the night with me? I'm not that cool a guy. At the club, you were not happy with my attitude and questions. So why?"

"At first, you were just another guy after me. Your questions were just an excuse to get close. It's happened too many times. But then I saw your concern looking for my brother's killer. You didn't even know he was my brother, but you cared. And mostly, I saw you weren't out to get me in bed. Everyone in that place was always making a pass. You didn't. You were different."

"If you remember, I did try to leave."

"I know. I know. That told me you weren't after me. You bought me dinner at the café. And you talked to me about nice things. Then you tried to take me home—to *my* home—so I asked to see your place. Like I said. You're different."

"Is being different all that's needed to get you in bed?" I asked, and immediately regretted it.

"Don't be an asshole." She was justifiably upset, again. And I was the jerk, again.

"I'm an asshole. Forgive my stupid, mean words. That was my detective side speaking, and I sometimes don't like that side. If you want to give me a knuckle sandwich, I promise not to duck."

"I'm sorry I called you that. What you are is a sweetheart. An honest one. You're sweet, kind, and caring. And I bet many a woman has felt that. And probably ended up in your bed." She was looking at me now with eyes wide and focused. Staring came to mind. "And I'm not going to hit you. If you want to spank me, you can." A welcome smile came to her lips.

I honored it with a kiss. "I think a light spanking might be needed, but that's for later. For now, we should get off the floor." When I got up she extended her hands. I took them and she rose until her arms were around my neck.

My case was moving in opposite directions. I must admit I liked this route, but it could be the more dangerous. She could be the killer, and I the next victim. She had just fed me. Time would tell. I was hoping to at least see the weekend.

She added, "Darling, I'm looking forward to tonight. For now, the kitchen calls me." With a brief kiss in the right place, that's where we went.

After giving me instructions on what to do, she washed, I dried.

She asked, "What are you doing today?"

"A little backtracking. Questions that need clearing up."

As she handed me a glass, she calmly asked, "Can I go with you?"

"No. That could put you in danger. You'd be seen as working with me and become a target."

She paused for a moment, put the saucer she was washing back in the sink, and faced me. She looked unhappy. "Are you a target?"

"Usually am. Comes with the territory."

"I don't like the territory," she uttered as she gave me the last cup to dry.

We needed a more pleasant subject. There was too much at stake with the one we were on. I gave her a little of my past, and she talked about her past as a singer. We finished the dishes and relaxed in the living room. The sofa provided better togetherness.

"I need you to tell me as much as you can about your brother." She gave me a tiny nod. "Did you ever go to his apartment?"

"Oh, yes. Often. We'd play cards, checkers, and just talk. We'd talk family and complain about our jobs. I'd fix him a meal sometimes when I was there. He always cleaned his plate."

She stopped for a moment. "I liked cooking for him." Her voice cracked, and she went silent. The fingers of one hand were caressing each other. If I could imagine, it seemed she was grieving over those times.

There were no words I could think of to match what she must have felt. She spoke of happier times. I offered what I could. "He was a good man. He deserved your attention." I paused briefly. "Tell me about your family. You said your parents were dead. How'd they die? Was your dad in the service?"

"We lived on a farm. Grew up on it. Daddy inherited it from his father. Daddy tried to enlist, but he had a bad eye. He would've made a good GI. Even with a bad eye, he was a good shot. He kept us supplied with fresh food. And fish. The Tennessee River has a lot less fish." She smiled sweetly as she remembered.

"He died in 1935. Doctors couldn't tell us why. Tommy was born in 1919. Mama had a stillborn in 1920. That had to be real heart breaking, but she didn't give up. She had me in 1921. Mama died in 1939. They said her heart just gave out. I've always thought she was just tired of living."

"Your mother had to be like mine, taking care of her family while living a tough life. Sounds like your dad was a good provider. What happened when he died?"

"Things got bad. The next year, we lost the farm. Tommy found us a shack to live in. I was sixteen and didn't know nothing. Dear God. Tommy had started working when he was ten. He milked cows on the farm. After Dad died, he milked for others, anyone. He delivered milk and anything to make a nickel." Tears were forming. "Sam, he became the man of the house. Why did he have to die? It's not fair."

"Life's not fair, so we just make the best of it. Your brother did that. Some are lazy and look to others for a handout. Tommy didn't. Looks like he took life by the horns and ran with it." I hoped she liked my take on Tommy's personality.

Delighted tears ran down her cheeks. She used a tissue from her purse sitting on the coffee table. "He did. You find who took him from me and kill 'em!" She stopped, realizing, I felt, what she'd said. "I can't believe I said that. Sam, I'm not like . . . Please forgive me?"

"You're forgiven. I'll find his killer."

She laid her soft hand on my cheek. "I know you will."

That felt nice, but . . . . "Let's move off that. We need to dry those tears. Do you have a key to his apartment?"

"Sure do. Why?" She seemed supportive.

"I'll need it when I go back to his apartment."

"Hey. You've *already* been to his apartment. You told me last night. How'd you get in?"

"Let's just say the door fell open for me." I said that with no expression, but I was caught.

"You picked the lock, didn't you?"

"I'd prefer to leave it as falling open due to my asking politely."

"You stinker, you picked the lock." She seemed happy that I did. Then, she returned my confession with a wicked grin, as she hit me with the back of her hand, not hard, you understand. One of those hits like girls do. With a wink, she slipped off the sofa and got her purse. Dropping back on the sofa and snuggling next to me, she retrieved her key chain and gave it to me, holding the apartment key for me to remove, which I did.

"I won't keep it long, but it could come in handy. Sometimes locks don't pay me any attention."

"If you go back, I'd want to go, too."

"I'll consider it. Tell me about his job." I attempted to slide away from her request.

"Well, he had a good job. He was a team leader for a construction company."

"Know the company?"

"Walker Construction. They have an office on Thirteenth Street. I've never been there. Tommy liked his job. Sometimes he didn't approve of some decisions, but management was good to all the guys. The pay was decent."

"Have they called you?"

"No. Why would they?"

"Some companies will contact relatives if an accident happens."

"I'm pretty sure Tommy didn't give them my phone or address. He would've told me."

"One thing is odd. Your brother's last name is Mitchell. Yours is Summer. Why?"

"You don't stop digging, do you? I didn't want the people at the club to know my real name. Charmers Club is not the most reputable place. But, I needed work and they hired me."

"And they tried to farm you out. Do you know if they did that with other women there?"

"They did. The girls don't like it, but they got no choice. When I told Tommy, he got real mad. He went after the management and was going to tell the police what they were doing to the girls. I didn't hear it all, but that's what he told me. Do you think someone at Charmers killed him?"

"Possible, but those types would usually take it out on you. They damage the unseen parts of the body, leave the face alone."

Her head began to shake wildly back and forth. And I had caused it. I pulled her close so that her chin was resting on my shoulder. She let her feelings out. "What have I done? No one told me that. Sam, I can't go back there."

"You've done nothing but try to find a good job. And no. You can't. Here." I needed to get her mind off that. I continued to hold her but moved her in front of me. She was a little calmer now. Giving her my pencil and notepad, I asked her to write the names she knew at the club. She also wrote if they were owners.

"Do they have your address?"

Her eyes opened wide. "Oh, God. They do. I had to give them my phone number, too. What am I going to do? I wish Tommy was here." She wrapped her arms around herself.

"Will I do?"

Her hands dropped to her lap. "You're perfect. I'll do whatever you want." She sounded calm, but for a moment she had been shaking.

I pulled her close to me. "I'm pretty sure no one followed us here last night. I took some precautions. Even my home phone shows my business address. You're safe here. And I think you need to stay here till I know more of who's involved."

She gently pulled away, and with her arms spread wide said, "I guess you know the only clothes I have are what you see."

"I liked them best when I couldn't see 'em." She hit me, again.

"Okay, Smarty. We're going to my apartment today and getting me some clothes. Is that understood?"

I liked her confidence. "Yes. Understood. We'll do that after dark. Now, with your permission, I'll visit the club and discuss your quitting."

"You do know how to move off topic. I'm going with you," she said without a quiver.

"You're not going. They will not see you again. They now know you're connected to Tommy. And they can't be sure what you might do now that he's dead. You could disappear."

Katie started to say something but I shushed her.

"You're staying here till I get back. I'm going by the police station to get a scoop on the club and its owners. Is that understood?"

"Yes. I guess so," she answered uncertainly.

"Now, listen close. I can keep you safe so long as you do as I say. If you go out on your own, you could get us both killed. Do I make myself clear?"

She tilted her head down, appearing to give in. "Yes," she said, those veiled blue eyes directed at me with pouting lips.

"I want your promise you will stay here *and* not contact anyone."

"I promise." She sounded more absolute. I knew I could only hope.

"I expect you to keep your word. After I've left, do not open that door for anyone but me. When I get back, I'll knock four times and say 'it's *not* me'."

"Okay. Please hurry back. I'll get lonesome." She almost clung to me.

I stood and told her I'd be heading for the police station. Which was true, but it would not be my first stop. The mystery sister, Lidia, needed my attention.

It was midmorning and Lidia heard knocking at her door. It was me. No surprise to you but . . . it was to her. I hadn't made an appointment, on purpose. I prefer a client's story be spontaneous. However, I too was in for a surprise—she had company. At least she was fully clothed, in case you were wondering.

"Mr. Marlow! Oh, ah, good morning." I was a bolt from the blue, but she managed to hide her astonishment well.

"Good morning, Lidia. May I come in?"

"Of—of course." As I walked in, she introduced me to her guest, possibly because I was staring at him. "Mr. Marlow, this is my friend, Henry Kilgore."

"Good morning. Didn't mean to barge in"—I extended my hand, which he took—"but I have some questions looking for answers." I turned to Lidia. "If I may?"

She said okay and directed me to a chair. She sat down beside Henry.

I broke the ice. "The police ain't finding much, and they ain't very forthcoming with what they know. Could you tell me just what you told them?"

"I already told you, Mr. Marlow," said Lidia, head tilted and eyes tight—wondering why I must have forgotten, I suspect. Of course, I hadn't, but both lies and truth can vary when repeated.

"I know, but with such a horrible thing that you experienced, people can forget, so it helps me with the case to have you go over it again. Hope you don't mind?"

"Oh, okay. Sure." She glanced at Kilgore, then continued. "I told them I'd come down from Virginia for a visit. Tommy had sent me a letter. Said he was lonesome. When I opened the door, I saw him lying there." She paused, covering her eyes, then stood up saying, "Excuse me," and got a tissue from the table to wipe her tears. As she sat back down she apologized.

I nodded.

Sniffing a little, she said, "It was . . . It was awful. That's when I called the police."

"I guess you checked to see if he was alive first? When we first talked, you didn't mention that."

"Oh, yes. I did. I mean, I didn't tell you, but I did see if he was alive. Well, I didn't check his pulse, but I squatted down and pushed on him a little. I didn't want to hurt him. Maybe I didn't touch him hard enough. Oh, I don't know. I was scared and, I think, afraid to do anything. When he didn't move, that's when I called the police. I didn't really know what else to do."

"Yes, I can understand the situation. I remember you told me you didn't have a key and that the door was open."

She turned to look at Kilgore. I wondered if it was for approval. Then to me, she said, "I do have a key, but I left it at home. And yes, the door was open just a tiny little bit, so I just opened it. I didn't expect anything wrong. When we were kids, we didn't lock our doors at home. I should have known better."

"That was a scary situation, and only a cop would really know what to do. You got the police there quickly. You did good. Now, let's get off that and talk about his past. Any specifics like jobs he's had or problems he got into?"

"Well, when he was young, he just did boy things. He didn't have to work. I don't remember any problems. He was a sweet guy. But since he moved down here, I don't know what all he was doing."

"I don't think I asked about your parents. Where do they live?"

Her hand slowly moved to Henry's leg. "Daddy's dead. I live with Mother up in Virginia. That's why I don't get down here much. But his letter sounded so lonesome I just had to see him."

"Could I see the letter? Sometimes the words can give some meaning to just how someone's feeling." When I asked that, she looked at Kilgore. Without words, his facial expression seemed to tell her how to answer my question. I've always found it interesting how a look can give direction.

"I'm sorry, Mr. Marlow. I left it at home. The police wanted to see it, too."

"If I recall, you called your mother, right?"

"Yes. That's right. I just had to. It broke her heart."

I expected Lidia to shed a tear or two as she spoke, but she didn't.

"One last question. When you got to the apartment, did the door just open without any obstruction? I mean, did it hit something and you had to push the door harder? I ask because sometimes a killer will leave a chair or box or piece of furniture to make the door hard to open. It's a warning someone's trying to get in."

"You know, you're right, Mr. Marlow. Yes. I had to push hard to open it. When I got in, there was a small ottoman behind it. After I called the police, I moved it out of the way."

Henry quickly looked at her. Although he was breathing, he appeared agitated, as he should have been. He already knew what I had just discovered.

"Perfect, Lidia. That's a good piece of information. Oh, don't mention that to the police. That's our secret for now."

"Oh, Mr. Marlow. That makes me feel so good. Like I'm really helping."

I thanked her, shall we say, carefully. And I purposefully did not look at Kilgore. He was looking at us both. I wanted to make her feel good, and she should, after telling me more than she knew. If there was an ottoman blocking the door, how'd the killer get out? Jump? From the sixth-floor window? You got it. She was lying.

It was time for the police station, again.

When I got to the station, I nodded at the secretary. She smiled and didn't try to stop me. I think the term would be I *marched* into Lieutenant Mark Griffin's office. He was a friend, kinda.

Before I could say good morning, he barked, "Marlow, don't you know how to knock?"

"So, how's your day going, Mark?"

"Was going great till about five seconds ago. I got enough troubles. What are you here for?"

"Just checking if you have any leads on the Mitchell case. All I'm finding are dark alleys."

The lieutenant didn't look happy. I figured it was me.

"Nothing," he replied. But he stopped. He looked like he was pondering something, possibly whether to kick me out.

"Well, I do have one thing I can share. We found five distinct sets of prints in his apartment. Mitchell, his sister, and three unidentified. By now, I suspect we'll also find yours. Oh, and one of the unidentified must be a woman's. Prints were small and all over the apartment. The other sets, I expect, are men's. The killer or killers, maybe."

"I think that woman's prints belong to a Katie Summer. I got a tip late yesterday."

The LT didn't seem as excited as I thought he would be. "A phone call would've been nice."

"Well, there's a related issue. I spoke to Miss Summer late last evening. Two things, both related. Seems she knew Mitchell really well. Went to his apartment a lot. Her prints would be all over the place. Second, she was a singer at a club, and her employer wanted her to be extra special nice to some clients. We both know what that means. She refused and showed up at my place."

"So, where is she? Marlow, you know this is where she should be. You, I could care less. Get her down here!"

"Before I do, I got a question for you." I handed Katie's list of names to Mark. "You got anything on any of those guys?"

"What kind of anything?"

"Rackets? Assaults? Complaints? Anything?"

He took the list. "Okay, let me look." He looked for a minute, then picked up the phone, dialed a number, and told Hargrove, a detective, to get in there.

"I take it Hargrove has the answer."

"Shut up, Marlow. I'll let you know when I know."

Hargrove came in. We didn't need introductions. Wasn't the first time we were palling around on a case. Mark gave him the list.

Hargrove's eyes opened wide. "Damn. Every name on this list has been in for questioning for one thing or another. Nasty group. You cross these guys and you vanish. Now, Henry Kilgore, he's their leader. He bails out the others when they get into trouble."

He took a hard look at me, then Mark. "What have they done now?"

My day just took a sharp turn off a cliff. Looking back and forth toward Hargrove and Mark, I knew I was about to piss them off. I had to. Katie could be in real trouble.

"Now, let me finish, because Katie Summer may be in danger. She worked at the Charmers Club. She gave me that list of names. Katie told me this morning she was Mitchell's brother. And from the rundown she gave me of their past and present, she sounds legit. I believe he was her brother. Mitchell was going to report Kilgore to you guys. If Kilgore connects her to Mitchell, she's for sure in danger."

Mark jumped in. "What the hell, Marlow? Damn, that's serious news. I oughta toss you in the clink."

"For once, I agree. But there's more. I visited Lidia Mitchell a little over an hour ago. Henry Kilgore was there. She said he was her friend. She gave a limited and totally different story about Mitchell. She was just flapping her lips. Lying. How would Kilgore be a friend when she supposedly lives in Virginia? That's a long way to travel."

Mark stood up. "We need to get Summer in here, NOW!"

"I'll go get her. You need to get Lidia, whatever her name is, and Kilgore. He could have his henchmen hanging around."

"Agreed. You get Summer down here fast."

I pulled Mark aside for one more favor and took off like a bullet. Until what I had just heard, I hadn't thought it was that bad. I was wrong. And the walls were closing fast.

I got back to my apartment in under twenty minutes. Katie wasn't there. The door was broken into and the lock was split off. My mind went over last night and today, but nothing clicked. Then I saw it. The phone's handset was off the hook, hanging down, barely swaying. I grabbed it by the cord and saw blood on the handset. Not much, but some. There was blood on the floor, too. Whoever took her, it had to have been within minutes. Maybe even two or three minutes. I took a quick look around the rooms, then one last look at the dangling phone, now still as a corpse, and left.

When I got in my car, I pulled an inconspicuous latch and retrieved my spare .38 from its hidden home under the dash. Figured it might come in handy.

Ignoring speed limits, I got to the club in under fifteen minutes. It wasn't open yet, so I circled around to the back door, slammed on the brakes, and almost jumped out of my car. Luck was with me—some guy delivering booze had the back door open. He yelled, but it was not a time to stop. My feet were running. After swerving through a couple of turns, I was at Kilgore's door.

I had no key. If I knocked, I was dead. Katie, too. A surprise visit was the answer. Without slowing, my left shoulder hit the door. It and my body fell into the room.

All I remember was rolling a couple turns, hearing Katie scream, and seeing her and two goons off to the side holding her. They pulled guns. One of them fired at the ceiling, the other at me. My leg hurt as I took another roll and fired back. I popped one somewhere. He went down. I took out the one trying to kill the ceiling, then hit something as I heard another shot. Things got blurry.

My fuzzy eyes opened and I found myself in a bed with white sheets in a room that smelled like a hospital. It was a hospital.

Then some sweet words caught my attention: "Hi, handsome. Glad you're back with us."

I remember asking, "Am I in a hospital, or a mortuary talking to an angel?"

"A hospital, silly. It's me, Katie, or have you forgotten me so quickly?"

This was a time a detective should know all the answers, but my memory had sprung a leak. "What happened?"

"You barged into Kilgore's office taking out the door and the two guys who took me from your apartment. A cop came in right behind you and shot Kilgore."

"Really?"

"Yes. Really. You were amazing."

"No. Someone followed us last night. I didn't cover our tracks very well. And that nearly got you killed."

Her smile disappeared. Then, she cried, "Oh, Sam," and her hands went to cover her mouth. "I didn't think . . . No, not you. I did it. I got up after midnight and called one of the girls I'm friends with at the club. I just had to tell someone about you. How special you were. I called her home number, but they must have found out. I did this. I'm so very sorry."

"Actually, I understand. It's not the first time something like that has happened. Don't worry about it."

Her attitude changed in an instant. "So, Sam, you've had other women in bed? That same bed!"

"No, not me. I'm talking about it happening to other clients." *Oh, shit. I best not lie.* "Would you mind asking the doctor to come back in here?"

"And why should I do that?" She was angry and waiting for an answer.

Attempting to look sick, I replied, "When I answer your question, I may need a gurney and a sheet."

"I want an answer or you will! Now speak!"

I spoke gently and calmly. "There've been one or two others, but it's been a long time. Really. And they were not like last night. Last night and this morning had a special feeling. One that I don't want to forget."

She was annoyed, but she smiled her forgiveness. She took hold of my hand. "Most men would have said I was the first, so I believe you. That same time was special for me, too. And you won't need a gurney."

Every thought brought my feeble mind closer to the present. A tense present. I remembered the phone. "The blood. The phone had blood on it. What happened?"

"Ah, you're feeling better. It's amazing what a little truth will do for a man."

I stuck my tongue out. She replied with her tongue. I gave her hand a gentle squeeze.

"Okay. When they broke through the door, I grabbed the phone thinking to call you. That was dumb. One of them grabbed my arm. I slapped at him and scratched his face. His icky blood was all over my fingers. It was under my fingernails! Then he hit me, and the floor came up to meet me. Least, that's what it felt like. I heard them laughing while I was lying there. When their laughing stopped, they picked me up and took me to Kilgore."

"Does it hurt?"

"It did, but the doc gave me something. It's better. I'm okay."

"I'm glad. So, why did the guy shoot the ceiling? Why do my head and leg hurt like hell?"

"Well, when I saw it was you, I pushed the guy's arm up as the gun went off. That got the other one distracted for a second. He then turned back and got off two shots, one in your leg and the other grazing your forehead. Guess that *second* gave you time to put one in his chest. The cop came running into the room and stopped Kilgore from doing anything. You stopped moving. I thought you were dead." She looked sad again.

"I was trying to save your life, and you saved mine."

She leaned over and gave me a kiss.

"You said you made the guy shoot the ceiling. That was a brilliant move. I'm not sure how many women, or *men*, would've thought of that."

"It was my dad. Daddy didn't just teach me how to be a lady. I was shooting a pistol by my seventh birthday. By age ten, I could take a running rabbit down in time for supper with his .22 rifle. Never did like shotguns. Hurt my shoulder." Her beautiful smile made me feel much better.

Amazed at her words, I just looked up at her and thought about what I wanted to do with her later. I won't go into more details. "Thank you" was all that came out.

"You're welcome. I thanked the cop who finished the job with a kiss."

"A kiss?"

"On his cheek, silly," she added with a grin. "And when the cop saw all that had happened, he burst out laughing. I didn't think it was so funny."

"Now, I remember. I asked the LT to send a cop with me, but I lost him somewhere."

"Yes. He was quite upset. Said you broke every traffic law on the books. You were running out of your apartment building as he pulled up. He couldn't keep up with you, but he caught up as you got to the club."

We were enjoying ourselves when the LT stopped by. I thought it was good timing on his part. "Hi, Miss Mitchell. How you doing, Sam?"

"I ain't dead thanks to this woman, here. And her name's Katie."

The LT got my drift. "We'll all be seeing a lot of each other due to this case. Maybe we should do first names?"

"I'd like that, Mark," Katie replied.

"Me too, Katie." At least I got that out of the way.

"Mark, I guess you've collected bodies by now?" I asked.

"Yep. We got 'em all. And the bullets they fired at you"—he then looked at her—"Katie, they match the one that killed your brother. We got him."

Katie gave him a tearful hug. "That means so much." I think he liked the hug, but he did seem a little embarrassed. The red face gave him away.

After they separated he looked at me. "Sam, the info you gave us is paying off. We arrested the manager and he's cooperating very well. They had one hell of a prostitution ring going."

Katie jumped in, fast and upset. "I knew the girls were not happy, but never thought that was going on. And please go easy on the girls. They were as afraid as I was. I told Kilgore no, and see what happened? They had no choice."

"I do understand, Katie, and will take that into consideration."

"Can you promise me that? I'll testify in their favor if that will help."

"It's not easy to promise, but I will do what I can. And if it goes to trial, I'll let you know."

"Thank you, Mark. That means a lot."

"Mark, what about Lidia? And why the devil would she hire me?"

"Ah, that's the real reason I came by."

I blurted out, "What? I thought you came to check on me." If he had, that would've been a minor miracle.

"Like I said," he grinned, ignoring me, "Lidia is Lidia Gardner. No relation to Kilgore, but to his attorney. Who, by the way, we also have in custody. And that is a key point."

Then, looking at Katie, he continued. "Your brother had taken out a will, and he unknowingly used Kilgore's attorney. And when his guys killed your brother, they also stole his copy of the will. They needed it for Lidia. Katie, that will left everything to you."

"Me!" Katie got excited but puzzled. "He never told me he had a will."

Someone had to ask, so I did. "Anything in the will of any value?"

"The will doesn't state anything in particular. But we just found he had a bank savings account of over twenty thousand dollars. And that would be included. That had to be why all this happened. Guess it seemed like an easy twenty grand."

She was no longer holding my hand. Her hands lay limp in her lap.

He added, "Keep in mind, they knew you as Summer, so they didn't make the connection right off. That's why Lidia hired Sam. According to the manager, they figured Sam might find a relative and they'd bump 'em off."

Katie got back in the game. "But, I didn't tell anyone at the club my real name."

I grabbed a hand. "Ah, but Katie, you did. They had your home address and phone number. Wouldn't take much checking to get your real name."

"That's exactly what they did, Sam. When you came to the club and started questioning Katie, they put two and two together and came up with a relative who had to be disposed of. And according to the manager, you were on that same disposal list."

I finally realized what my own snooping had caused. Looking at Katie, I said, "And all because I found that picture. Talk about sheer luck. And bad luck at that."

Mark added his words to my words: "You better be glad you found that photo. And you're lucky Kilgore's goons didn't. If you hadn't gotten involved, they most likely would have figured it out anyway, and this lovely woman would've had no protection."

She looked at me and squeezed my hand. "He is a special guy."

"That's all I got for now. I need to get back to the station. You two hang loose till we get all this in its place." Saying that, he started out the door. Katie grabbed him and planted one of her kisses on his cheek.

He was almost out the door when I gave him a warning. "Hey, Mark! You might want to wipe off that red lipstick before Mrs. Mark sees ya."

Possible wifely fear grabbed him as he headed down the hall, while Katie and I laughed.

Katie moved a chair beside the bed. She sat on the bed with her silk stocking–covered feet in the chair.

"No idea what we were talking about." I figured a little kidding was in order. "Miss Nurse, I need an update. Guess my head's okay. Least I can talk. How's my leg?"

"Your head's fine. Doc said it just took off a few hairs. The leg's okay, too. It will take a few weeks of staying off it to heal up, so the doctor said."

"Will I need a nurse?"

"I volunteered. I don't have a job anyway. The doc told me everything I needed to know. If I missed anything, I'll make up the rest."

"Getting well will be fun. Course, I may never get well. It'll be nice to have you stop by every day."

"You said a little bit ago that last night and this morning had a special feeling that you didn't want to forget. Did you mean that?"

"Yes. And I can't recall ever feeling that way. Yes. I meant it. From the moment I started talking to you last night, you began to grow on me."

"Mark, I'm going to do something that my parents would be against and that your parents and no one will like. People will call me a slut. Daddy taught me how to protect myself, but it took more than me. Tommy died protecting me, and I now have a new, special memory of him. You nearly died for caring so much you did whatever you could for me. Now, listen carefully. If—If it's okay with you, I want to move in with you. Live with you. You see, I love you. I don't care if you never marry me. I just want to be with you. If you want me—"

I interrupted her. "Give me one of those bandages over there," I asked, pointing. She looked worried and brought me one. I stripped it down to the sticky parts.

"Katie, give me your left hand." She did and got quiet. "I love you. Will you marry me?" I kept it short. My leg hurt.

She said yes, and I put the bandage on her ring finger. She jumped. I couldn't see her feet, but I think they left the earth. When she came down, she bent over me and gave me a long one right on the kisser. My leg didn't hurt as much. I got distracted.

Well, that's it. That's my story. I'm still a gumshoe, and I now got a helper. Got me a woman. And to top it off, she's a dreamboat with great gams!

Oh, you may be asking how I knew where she was. Remember the icky blood? When I turned and walked around the phone table that last time, I saw the letter K written lightly on the floor, as you now know, with the goon's blood. K equaled Kilgore.

THE END of One Case and . . .

Uncle Allen and the Doll

The Sunday started as any other Sunday. The sun, sheltered by the wispiest of clouds, was still bright at late afternoon. The family gathered once again to eat, tell stories, and enjoy each other's company. As the day ended and the others left, Uncle Allen, the oldest family member, gave young Margaret a doll. He told her the doll was passed down from chosen child to chosen child. Margaret took the doll and sat down to play with no understanding of the new toy's special meaning. She was only three. Her mother was proud of her brilliant daughter, for she had started a chain reaction that would reach beyond their small town, maybe beyond Margaret's future.

Months went by. The years faded behind her. Margaret was now twenty-three and had grown into a beautiful woman. Men were constantly asking for dates. She dated them but resisted their charms when they got too serious. But for some reason, that attention slowly ceased.

In those twenty years, Uncle Allen and all her aunts and uncles had died. So had her father and mother. On her deathbed, her mother told her to remember the doll. Margaret said she would, but soon forgot. She was the last of her family and now alone.

One day while searching for her mother's diary, she found it. The Doll. It had not aged, not even a scratch or tear of its clothing. Because her mother had thought so much of the doll, Margaret put the doll on her nightstand as a reminder of her mother.

Margaret had been working many odd jobs: secretary, grocery clerk, and other jobs that were going nowhere. As soon as she found some girls to be friends with, they changed jobs, moved, or got married. She was still alone.

She now worked as the receptionist for a real estate agency, and Ben, one of the agents, she liked, but he showed her no personal attention. He was always nice and polite, and single, but only business. She managed to get a photo of him without his knowing. She printed a copy and laid it on her nightstand, trying to be close to him. More days went by with no luck.

At night she cried and, before going to sleep, talked out loud to him to ask her out.

It was a Friday and she was patiently waiting to leave at 5:00 p.m. when Ben stopped by and asked if she would have dinner with him that night. He apologized for such short notice but said he wanted to get to know her better.

She said yes, and the dinner with a movie following was great. He took her to her apartment and before leaving asked if she was busy Saturday afternoon. There was an old movie at the theater and he would like to see it with her. She was excited. They went and it was much fun.

They later sat in the park and watched the fountain bubble and kids splashing the water with their hands.

They began dating regularly. Her life was pleasant, till one day Ben told her that he must move to Denver. The company was opening a new office and they wanted him to manage it. It was a great opportunity.

She told him once he got it going that maybe she could move there with him. He said it could be a year or more before that would happen. Margaret almost begged him not to go, but he said he had no choice. If he refused, the management would probably let him go. It would be a month before he had to go, and they could still see each other. Ben took Margaret home. She kissed him at the door but wanted to be alone for now.

It was time to cry again. She threw herself on her bed and cried. This time she didn't talk but yelled at the company for making him go. Ben could make the Georgia company do good. The Georgia manager should go to Denver. Again she cried herself to sleep.

The next few days were suspenseful. Ben hadn't talked to her much, and he had not told her when he was actually leaving.

Finally, Ben stopped at her desk. "Looks like I'm staying here. They're sending someone else to Denver."

"I know you wanted to go and you would have made it successful, but I must admit I'm glad you are staying."

"Margaret, I'm not staying. I'm going anyway. I don't like it here and it will be better for me in Denver."

She was somewhat shocked, but wouldn't let it get between them. "When you go, I'll go, too." But that's when the true shock came.

"You can't go. I'm going alone. I have someone waiting for me there. I'm going to marry her."

"Ben, how could you do this? I thought you cared about me. You've been leading me on. You're a two-timing—" But she couldn't finish expressing her feelings. He'd drained the love from her heart. She told him to get away from her and never speak to her again.

She left work as soon as she could and went home crying. She threw herself on her bed, crying and wishing him dead, and the same for his Denver girlfriend. Margaret knew she should not have said that. It wasn't like her, but she was so very angry.

Weeks went by. She was slowly getting Ben out of her emotions. One Monday, her manager told the staff that Ben and his new wife had been killed in an auto accident. There were tears flowing from many, including Margaret.

With that tragedy, she began to see something in what she wished or asked for. Did she have some supernatural power? Surely not. She had feelings like any other person. But still, so much that she had wanted had happened. If she did have some power, how did it work? And it could be dangerous, and maybe even evil. She had to know more.

While sitting at her desk, she quietly wished that her manager would have a little fender bender going home, nothing serious, no one hurt.

The next day came and her manager arrived at the office. He said hello as usual. She asked how he was and if all was okay. As soon as she could sneak out, she went and looked at his car. Perfect. No damage. She tried asking some other things while in her car, in her kitchen, at church even, but nothing happened. Then it dawned on her. Her bedroom! Where all the crying took place.

She got home, went straight for the bedroom, and lay down on her bed. But what to do? How to do it? Ah, today's heading, that was it.

She simply made a statement, out loud: "They will find the little boy who is missing tomorrow morning, safe, healthy, and unharmed." With that done, she fixed supper and went to bed without saying another word.

The next day, she went to the break room at lunch and watched the TV, and there it was. They found the little boy safe and unharmed. With that success, she tried twice more. Both were successful. She then knew that she and the doll had the ability to make things happen.

It was now late evening. She began to remember how proud her mother always was of her and that Uncle Allen somehow knew she would have the gift to use the doll. Or maybe it was a partnership. Maybe it was the combination that made it possible. She knew she had caused the death of two people, and that would not happen again.

She went to bed. She knew why Uncle Allen and her mother had placed so much importance on the doll.

It was time to predict the future.

"Send me the right man that together we will love each other, live long, healthy lives, and have three children, all girls and all with special gifts to care for their families, for us, and for the future."

The Future Ending

Dark Meeting

The room was totally dark. No light was visible anywhere. That meant the curtains were pulled. The hall lights had been deliberately extinguished somehow. Mike took a few tentative steps into the room. The message had said nine o'clock, Room 17, Lincoln Hotel.

A low, raspy voice growled in the darkness behind him. "Hiya, Mike."

Mike jumped slightly, but the shadowy figure waiting for him couldn't see it.

"Trying to be scary, Frank?" asked Mike as he turned to face the voice, his host.

Frank pushed the door closed, then moved forward, farther into the room.

Mike turned slowly, following muffled footsteps. They were no more than two feet apart and could barely see each other's outline.

"Yeah. An' I scared ya, didn't I, Mike? Didn't I?" He was excited, almost laughing.

It didn't take much for Mike to regain his composure. "You haven't scared anybody but old ladies in a long time."

Frank made his living pulling worn-out tricks on unsuspecting tourists and spinsters with a little larceny in their hearts. He was always looking for the big one. He always came up short. But this time, he had struck pay dirt.

Mike already knew why he had been summoned. Frank had managed to kill a courier with top-grade counterfeit plates.

"I know why you called me here. I know you have the plates. And you're the one who's scared," Mike said as he gestured at the darkness.

"Me? Naw, I ain't scared," Frank said as he shuffled in place. "Just cautious. Yep, that's me, cautious." When Mike didn't say anything, Frank just let the silence linger. "Say . . . how'd you know I had the plates?"

"I have my sources."

"Yeah, and that's why I gotcha here. I figure you can find a buyer for me, uh, for us. We can split the take, seventy-thirty . . . uh . . . no, sixty-forty. I got the goods. You got the contacts. We can make a bundle."

"You're a fool, Frank. That little rube you whacked to get the plates was just a carrier, a delivery boy, a nobody. You stole the best fifty-dollar plates ever been made, from people who want them back. And those people will get them back. If you ain't sweating, you should be."

Frank *was* getting nervous. He never did have much nerve. The man he killed had made a mistake, turned his back just once too often.

"Hey, Mike, old friend. Come on, you can help me out here. Help us out." Frank's voice was beginning to shake. He smiled a smile no one could see and uttered a nervous laugh.

"The only way you're going to get out of this alive is to give me the plates. I'll return them to their owners. You know I don't lie. I don't have to. You know that. I am trying to save your life. Now, give me the plates."

"Oooh, no. I ain't giving you the plates till you promise to make us a deal. These things must be worth half a mil."

"They're worth a great deal more, but there's only one deal. I return the plates. You live."

"Hey . . . buddy . . ." Frank said, then his tone changed, the smile leaving his face. "You disappoint me. I thought you'd help me. But go on. Get outta here. I'll find a taker. You'll see. And I'll keep all the profit, too."

"Sorry you feel that way." Mike moved to the door and opened it. Standing in the doorway, Mike made a half turn and looked back in at the almost-invisible, dark frame facing him.

"See ya, Frank." Then he pulled the door to and left.

Mike was waiting at the end of the hall when he heard two muffled pops and something hitting the floor. The door of Room 17 opened and a shadowy figure moved toward Mike.

"I don't like doing things that way," said Mike.

"You had no choice and you know it."

"Did you get the plates?" asked Mike.

"Yep. The jerk never knew I was there."

The Terminal End

Drone Delivery
A Jesse Falcon Mystery

It was a regular Saturday morning for families in Marietta subdivisions. Barbeques starting in backyards, lawn mowers collecting trimmed grass, and a drone dropping a body. Not to mention fourteen 911 calls.

Jesse hurried into the chief's office wondering, *Why the urgency?* He had stopped by the office to pick up an old file he was researching.

"Last time I'll stop by here on a Saturday. What's happening?"

"You are not going to believe this," the chief started. "We got fourteen 911 calls that a drone dropped a body on a lawn in a subdivision off Whitlock."

Jesse quipped, "Sounds special delivery."

"Ha. Ha. Look, I know this is your day off, but I really need *you* there. And fast. It's a very upper-class community and I don't know what you'll run into. This is so bizarre I need you to investigate it. Our guys and the medical examiner are probably there by now."

"Have you called Dan? He lives out that way."

"I called you first, then Dan and Bobby. Dan may already be there. I left Bobby a message.

"Thanks, Chief. I'm on my way."

When Jesse got to the scene, Dan was there. So were the crowds gathering on every lawn in sight. These were two-story homes, some with three- and four-car garages, and most equipped with basements.

Dan gave Jesse all he had learned thus far. He had names, addresses, and contact details. Some of the neighbors had looked at the body before the police had arrived, but they were moved back to keep the crime scene somewhat undisturbed.

The medical examiner finished up and told Dan and Jesse it was a male, late forties. The ME would do more tests in the lab because the body did not look as expected. He told Jesse and Dan the man was dead before he hit the ground.

The ME and the body left.

"Is Bobby going to be here to help?" asked Dan.

"Yep, the chief left Bobby a message. Probably with Susie. He'll be along. Course, if he's with Susie, who knows."

"And he drives me crazy singing that ancient song 'If You Knew Susie Like I Know Susie.' But I can't blame him."

They both had a laugh over that one.

Dan and the police had already identified fourteen people who had heard and seen the actual drop. They all told close to the same story. The drone had moved into the neighborhood, hovered a few seconds, and deposited the body. They described the man as looking facedown, arms spread wide and feet together all flat up under the drone.

No one could identify the body. Everyone denied taking pictures. But neighbors were still in their yards. It was time for Jesse and Dan to talk to the witnesses again before they vanished.

Jesse gathered seven witnesses who were handy. They told Jesse and Dan the same they had already heard. But Jesse needed more. It was time for fresh details.

He started, "I need to know the time the body was dropped, what direction the drone came from, and the direction it went after it dropped the body."

A hand went up. Jesse recognized the hand.

"I'm Bill Basehart. We've already told the other officers, but I know you guys have to ask again. I live right over there. We were in the backyard when we heard it. It came directly over us and straight across the street. It was coming from the south. We took off for our front yard and saw it drop the man in Sam Garfield's yard at about eleven, then it headed north."

Dan asked, "You are sure it headed north?"

"Oh yes. It headed up that street. Due north into the Kennesaw Park." Mr. Basehart pointed to Oak Street. "In no time, it was out of sight into the trees."

Dan thanked him then said, "Does anyone have a different viewing of that? Maybe what you saw looked different? Maybe you saw a strange car in the neighborhood? Just have to ask."

No hands went up. They only shook their heads no.

Jessie continued. "We've been told that no one could identify the body. Could the deceased be a resident of your subdivision?"

More shakes, then one woman who identified herself as Mrs. Jones confirmed, "We have street parties several times a year and HOA meetings. Stonehenge Court is a small community. If he lived here, we would know him."

Jessie asked, "Is the owner of the house where the body was dropped present?"

Mrs. Jones chimed in again, "They're on vacation. A river cruise in Europe."

"Thanks, Mrs. Jones," Jesse continued. "I'll have my team try to contact them. Did any of you get a picture of the drone?"

More heads twisted side to side.

Jesse asked for Garfield's contact information, which Mrs. Jones said she would provide. He then thanked the group for their help and added that he might have more questions as the case continued. With that the group dispensed. The street and lawns were now clearing swiftly.

Jesse could not believe with mobile phones in everyone's pocket no one had taken a picture.

"Dan, did you get the impression that the residents think the man was alive and died when he hit the ground?"

"Yes. Before you arrived, one of the women asked me why anyone would kill someone that way. Before I could answer, one of the men said that some people are just mean and evil. That seems to be the impression these people have."

"Let's keep it that way. Dan, you know drones. You fly those things. Could one be big enough and quiet enough to haul a body?"

Dan had been flying drones, the smaller versions, for a couple of years.

"The military drops bombs with drones all the time, but drones are not typically that large in the private sector. But it is certainly possible. I suspect this one had four engines. It would probably rotate to allow steady up-and-down movement and pause to drop the body, then burn rubber outta here."

"Strange that no one seemed to hear it coming any sooner. Dan, surely they had to have heard something?"

"With battery-powered engines or even the right gas-powered engines, it would make very little sound, if only a steady whirring. As to pictures, I agree. People of all ages have a phone in their shirt pocket, in a hip pocket, a clip on the belt. And the younger crowds are constantly taking pictures. Basehart's family had some kids there, but claimed they didn't take any pictures. I also think that is odd."

"Yeah. Somehow it doesn't fit."

Dan continued. "Whoever was guiding the drone could have been miles away. They could have done this from their living room. I hear they will soon be delivering pizzas by drone. Now, controlling the drone would take two hands, so if there was a vehicle involved, there was also a driver. They had to see where it was headed. There had to have been a camera on board."

Jesse began to speculate. "Seems it would've taken at least two individuals to get the body hooked to the drone. And that's really a maybe. From there one person could fly it, drop the body, and get rid of the drone, right?"

"Yes. I'll do some digging and see what engineering firms could build a large drone. If this baby was moving fast, I need to start tracking. I'll take a couple of blues and start asking around the area moving north. If it stayed in the park's trees, that will widen the search area. Quiet or not, it had to come out of the trees somewhere, and someone had to have at least seen it."

"Yeah, I agree. Better get two teams together. Let me know if you need more and I'll call the captain. I'll get Amy to contact the owner on that cruise."

Dan left to get his teams started.

Jesse's phone started singing. It was Rachel, the new Mrs. Falcon.

"Hi, beautiful. And I have no idea when I'll get home."

Rachel had heard that many times. "I understand. I'll tell the Markhams we'll have to reschedule. They won't mind."

"But will *you* mind?"

"Sweet, I understand. No complaints from me. Well, so long as you get home before midnight, maybe? I promise you *will* be rewarded."

After a pair of "I love yous" came a pair of clicks.

One of the remaining officers joined Jesse. "Stu, any ID on the deceased yet?"

"Just got it. A William Warren. Address is in Peachtree City. Single. Age fifty-two. Prelim says he was a manager with an engineering firm, Turbo Tech Controls. That's strange."

"What's strange?"

"Well, he lives in Peachtree City, but the business address is in Kennesaw. That is a *very* long commute." Stu and Jesse both nodded on that one. "And the name sounds very familiar. I'll continue to dig."

Jesse was getting bits and pieces, but he knew there must be a link. "There must be a connection to the residents and where the body was dropped. If you hear anything, let me know."

He got a "Will do," and Stu went back to his car and left.

"Excuse me," said a young girl as she walked up to Jesse. "I'm Maggie Parker, we live next door to where the body was dropped. I got to thinking about something that you need to know."

Jesse wanted any details he could find from anyone, even from this maybe-sixteen-year-old wearing very short shorts.

"I'm Jesse Falcon, and I am definitely interested."

Maggie smiled and continued.

"I was outside in my front yard when the drone came over the Basehart's house. It seemed like it was unsure what to do. I mean, it sorta hovered over the street for several seconds, then moved to Mr. Garfield's yard. About then is when the neighbors all came to their yards."

"Sorta hovered?" asked Jesse.

"Well, it seemed to move sideways just enough to notice. I mean, when I first saw it, it was steady over Mr. Basehart's yard. Then it moved to the street, did the sideways, then moved to Mr. Garfield's yard and dropped the body."

"Maggie, two questions: What time did you see the body drop? And, anything specific or unusual about what you saw?"

"The body dropped right about eleven, at least by my watch. Mr. Falcon, someone must have been electronically guiding the drone. They would have to be close enough to see where to do the drop, right?"

Jesse commented, "The guider had to have that visibility or another means of seeing it. And if the guider did a bad job, the body just might be on the wrong lawn."

"But Mr. Falcon, why would anyone want to kill a man that way?"

"I've been thinking about that, too. From what you saw, the question is, Did the body get dropped on the right lawn? Wherever it should have been dropped, it was dropped there for a reason. And if it should have been dropped on Basehart's lawn, then the reason is associated with him or his family. My choice for the connection is now Garfield or Basehart."

"But how can you figure that out?"

Jesse knew there might be some gossip around.

"Maggie, I'm going to ask you something, and you do not have to answer it."

She was a little skeptical, but wanted to help. "Ask away."

"I know that families do gossip with family members and between neighbors, and that gossip spreads. Are you aware of any problems that Basehart and Garfield or their families have? I'm just looking for a connection."

Maggie smiled, not so much that the answer might be funny, but that she could be spreading gossip herself. "Mr. Falcon, I did hear that Mr. Basehart was having some business problems, or maybe it was money problems. His daughter, Peggy, told me something last month. She wanted a new car, and he said she couldn't have one right now. He's bought her three cars over the last four years. He has—or had—the money."

"And suddenly he couldn't. Maggie, that's a start. I really appreciate all you've told me. If you hear anything more, please tell me. And let's keep it our little secret till I narrow it down a bit."

"I will. Oh, there's one more thing. Would you like a picture and a short video of the drone?"

Surprised, he nodded with a pleased smile. "Would I?"

He gave her his phone number and she texted it to him. "Maggie, this is great. This will be very helpful. Say, could I have your dad's name? Just for reference."

Maggie offered a very nice smile, her hands clasped behind her back. "Sure. My dad's name is Franklin Taylor. Mr. Falcon, this is sad but exciting. I'm glad I could help."

She turned to leave, then did a rolling turn while walking backward to give Jesse a smile and a "See ya!" as she turned to head home.

Jesse fired off the picture and video to Dan just as Bobby showed up. He had been at the local hospital. His girlfriend was a nurse there. When Jesse gave him the rundown and mentioned *drone*, Bobby jumped in.

"Boss, I've been at the hospital with Susie for most of the morning. At about eleven thirty, blues brought in two guys: both shot; one dead, one close to it. They were fishing on Lake Sunrise. You know, that new lake off Whitlock. The park security found them after they heard some noise. They were on the backside of the lake, where they were not supposed to be. All that is a bit sketchy right now, but when they brought in the fishermen, I was there with Susie. The live guy looked up at me and I leaned down close to him, and he said, 'Drone,' and I know right where they were fishing." Bobby smiled brightly.

"Bobby, that's gotta be our first lead. The body was dropped at eleven. I double confirmed that. Dan and his officers are tracking down any witnesses that may have seen the drone. I was told it headed north, but all it needed was a sharp right and the lake would be very close. Call Dan. You guys meet where they were fishing. Dan can backtrack and see if our drone here is the same drone the fisherman saw. You stay at the drone site and get some divers over there. I think our evidence is soaking."

Bobby saluted Jesse, pulled out his phone, and headed for the lake.

Jesse called the chief and told him what he knew. Because of the connection between the drone drop and the lake murders, the chief put him in charge of all investigation teams. Jesse then called Dan and Bobby with that info. Now they had large team working together.

But Jesse was still missing a connection. Then the light blinked. That's the one that blinks when your mind finds a path. When Rachel's uncle was alive, she had mingled with the upper crust all around Marietta. And for that matter, Jesse knew she still did. And that she had often run errands for her uncle, and she might know of connections to the families he was now dealing with. Jesse pulled his phone and tapped her number.

"Hey, sweet. You got good news for me?" she asked as she answered the phone.

"Ah, no, sweetheart, I'll get home as soon as possible. But I need your help."

"If it will get you home even today, just ask."

"You know about the drone body drop, or I'd be at home with you."

Rachel slipped in, "You really didn't have to remind me."

"I know, but it gets interesting. There were also two fishermen shot at Lake Sunrise not long after the drone drop. The body was dropped in Garfield's yard, but sources here think the drone may have made a mistake. Maybe the body was supposed to drop in Basehart's yard. I need to find a connection as to why the body was dropped in either of those yards. Can you help?"

Rachel wouldn't admit it much, but she did like to help. "Sure. Give me some names."

"Here are the names: William Basehart and Sam Garfield. They live here across the street from each other. Franklin Taylor Parker lives one house down. William Warren, the dead man, lived in Peachtree City but worked in a technical firm in Kennesaw. Basehart has lots of money, or did, but may be having financial problems. See if you can find any connection in the upper crust to any of those."

"Now watch that 'upper crust.' Remember, till I married you, I was crusty."

"Ah, but you were the beautiful, delicious icing, never crusty."

Rachel liked that. "Okay, you're forgiven, assuming you ever get home to lick the icing."

"Sweetheart, this could be a difficult case to crack, but I promise to get home as soon as I can."

"I know you will, sweetie. I'll make some calls and see what I can find on these names. Cobb has a lot of wealthy subdivisions, very crusty. Now you got me saying it. I don't recognize the names, but my Uncle AJ knew everyone. Sometimes I've thought he kept a dossier on all the crusties."

With more "I love yous," they ended the call.

Information was drying up at the scene. Drone escaped, pictures taken, body gone, and with the neighborhood trying to regain some normalcy, Jesse headed for the lake.

The lake seemed peaceful enough. The back of the lake was up against the Kennesaw park property, and that's where Bobby had said the men were fishing. Dan called

Bobby and told him he had found several locations where the drone had been seen, and two of those locations confirmed a hard right to the water. They had the connection. Bobby had already called in a diving crew, and they had suited up and started searching underwater. The game was on.

The why remained anonymous. Jesse was centering on the assumption this was some sort of a grudge or warning to someone in that subdivision. But why the adult-size drone? A letter with ricin or a package with a bomb would be much cheaper with the same result. A drone was not a cheap reminder. Why not just dump the body on the lawn during the wee hours? Someone was making a point. An expensive point. A very drone point. While he was pondering, his phone chimed.

"Jesse here."

"This is Stu. William Warren is deceased."

"Stu, we know that."

"Very true, but he died two weeks ago . . . and was buried. Jimmy Keeler worked the case, which they've closed. Seems Warren was driving fast and his car went out of control, ran off a bridge on I-75, and was literally crushed. Seat belts didn't do any good. Jimmy got very interested when I told him what we had, and I told him I'd keep him updated."

Jesse remembered that case. "Ah, I remember that. The car flipped over. And yes, keep him in the loop. But let's keep all this as quiet as possible. This is an odd connection." Stu agreed and hung up. Another question continued to bug Jesse: Why no pictures?

He called Maggie back and asked her if she knew of anyone else taking pictures.

"Sure," said Maggie. "Mr. Basehart's children, Benny and Sheryl, both had their phones aimed on it when they came running from the backyard. I saw them myself. But Mr. Basehart said something to them and they put their phones away."

Another puzzler for Jessie. "Maggie, when I asked about pictures, no one spoke up. No one. And Basehart's wife and others were there."

"But his kids did take pictures. Believe me, I saw them."

"I believe you. I just have to find out why Basehart wants to keep it a secret. Oh, did the police interview you or your mom or dad? I got there late, so I just wanted to know."

"No. When I went inside, Mom had some dinner started, so I was helping her till I saw you. And Dad just got home a little while ago. I told him about the drone. Mr. Falcon, have you figured why anyone would drop a dead body on anyone's lawn?"

Jesse paused. "Not yet, but some pieces are coming together. You've been a big help. Guess I better get going. Thanks again."

"Goodbye, Mr. Falcon. Call me anytime."

Information was traveling fast. Jessie had just learned that pictures had been taken. Then Dan called and told him that on Maggie's video he had seen Basehart's kids taking pictures, then Basehart had looked angry and told them to stop. This confirmed what Maggie had told him.

Jesse would need to talk with Basehart again, but he wanted more details that he hoped Rachel might find.

It took about two hours for the divers to find the soaking evidence. Drone delivered. Jesse was watching them bring up the drone when Rachel called.

"Hi, sweetheart. Good timing, they just pulled up the drone."

"Oh, you found it. Now get ready for my news," said Rachel with a big smile that beamed right out of the phone. Jesse was also smiling.

He signaled for Bobby to get near and listen.

"I like this FaceTime stuff you taught me. You look beautiful, especially to these tired eyes."

"Well, give 'em a rest and use your ears. Uncle AJ came through. Get this. Basehart, Garfield, Parker, and Warren are all related," she started, and without letting Jesse get a word in edgewise, she continued. "They all work for Turbo Tech Controls. That company makes software and devices that control," she paused for effect, "drones."

All Jesse could get in was a "What?" and a puzzled look.

Rachel continued. "Basehart is the CEO, Garfield is the company attorney, and Parker is a VP of engineering. I don't know how Uncle AJ knew, and I did not ask, but his contacts told him that a company designer stole drawings related to drone propulsion and some new-type software that can control a drone someone else is controlling. Oh, I know that doesn't make sense. I didn't understand it all, but it allows someone to control any electronic thing that is connected to the Internet. I think I got that right. Okay, your turn."

That was enough to alert Jesse to get Dan involved, whom he called over. His team was now a trio. Rachel repeated. Dan listened. They went back and forth. Jesse and Bobby just listened.

Dan threw out his thoughts: "Rachel, when you are buying groceries and errands in your minivan, do you listen to the radio?"

"Sure, Dan. You guys know I need noise all the time and love XM. Why do you ask?"

Dan was on a roll. "Rachel, your radio connects to the Internet to get the music. And your car and all newer cars are just big laptops. Jesse, I remember now that when Warren died, there didn't seem to be a reason for him to drive off that bridge. No history of heart trouble. Very good health, not that old. The accident wasn't traffic related. Suicide came up, but his friends all said that was not possible. Remember that, Jesse?"

"I do. It was finally logged simply as an accident."

"Right. Now, suppose you have software and a drone to hack into a car's system via the Internet, and through their radio, cause the car to speed up or make a sudden turn off a bridge. No one would ever know."

Rachel chimed in, "Guys, this is a little over my head, but it sounds possible. And if you had some reason to kill someone, that would make it undetectable, right?"

It was Jesse's turn. "That puts Basehart at the top of the list for murder. Maybe the attorney, Garfield, knew it. Or better yet, Parker knew it. And maybe Parker . . . Okay, this is another connection. When Maggie, Parker's daughter, first made contact with me, she said, and I quote, 'Why would anyone want to kill a man like that?' Her father was not home at that time. Later when I called Maggie, she said her father had gotten home. She then said, and I quote, 'Why would anyone drop a dead body on anyone's lawn?' It was a *live* body, then it was a *dead* body. The neighbors did not know the body was dead. Someone changed her mind."

The trio expounded, "*Her father.*"

Jesse queried, "But why?"

Rachel picked it up.

"I think the ball is in my court. Uncle AJ said that Mr. Warren and Mr. Parker were good friends. They had worked together for years. If Parker figured Basehart killed his friend, would he be angry enough to do this? But to dig up his friend's body. That's sick."

Jesse had the ball again. "Talk about getting very connected. Dan, get search warrants for the offices of all three, Parker, Garfield, and Basehart, as well as their homes, doing Parker's last. And Bobby, tell Stu and Jimmy. Guys, we're paying Parker a visit."

Jesse, Dan, and Bobby with backup called on the Parkers that afternoon. When they arrived, Parker came out to meet them. "I knew you would be coming. I've prepared my family."

Maggie had already been crying, and when she saw Jesse come in, the tears started again. Once all were inside and seated comfortably, Jesse gave his findings and conclusion that Parker had dug up his friend's body, William Warren, and dropped it on Garfield's yard, which, as expected, was by mistake.

Parker admitted to everything. He knew he would be prosecuted for his acts, but his point had been made. Parker admitted there was a prototype drone his friend knew about and the damage it could do. Warren could only take the existing drawings, hoping that would delay the final product. With the evidence found and testimony provided by Garfield, the attorney, and Parker, along with the police investigation, it was enough to convict Basehart of murder. But Parker was not off the list.

Two men had been killed. Parker admitted he had had an accomplice flying the drone. When they had neared the lake, Parker had left, leaving the controlee there alone, who had then killed the two fishermen because they had seen him and the drone. Parker would not get off easy.

With the day pretty much history, Jesse and Rachel, Bobby and Susie, and Dan and his girlfriend, Kati, went to dinner at a local café, then to the Brew with a View above the Strand Theater. Through dinner and now with brew in hand they could not stop talking about the case.

"Dan," started Jesse, "you called it. The drone hacked Warren's car through the radio connected to the Internet. I must admit, I would not have thought of that."

"Until it gets more widely known," Dan started, "no one would have given it a thought. It's been on the news, but we have to realize our cars are now computers, and computers can get hacked just like a laptop. The scary part is we don't know what criminal minds are already doing research. Not everyone watches the news."

Rachel smiled an *I told you so* as she spoke. "Well, I watch the news, and I told Jesse about drones that can hack a car through the radio. And that was months ago. But he never listens to anything I say."

That got a laugh from everyone except Jesse.

"Sweetheart," Jesse began, "I do listen to what you tell me. *Really*. You're my favorite reporter."

"Sure, and it goes in one proverbial ear and out the other. But Jesse, darling, I still love you."

Bobby looked up, pointing. "That plane is flying slow and low. It's headed right over the square."

No sooner than he got the words out, a body fell out of the plane and landed right on the fountain. The girls and many others around them screamed. Families in the square were running in all directions. The pointed top of the fountain protruded through the body.

"Guess our next case just dropped in," said Bobby.

Point Well Taken

Fogged
A Jake Stone Mystery

—⚮—

The plane circled over Jackson for an eternity, waiting like an expectant father for the fog to lift. The small, rectangular windows used to view the skyworld were covered with white cotton. No lightning. No thunder. Fog everywhere.

The flight attendants completed their final landing duties. They had already served soft drinks to the coach cabin, and wine, hard liquor, and soft drinks to first class. Blake noticed the white, condensed air boiling from the vent near the galley.

He knew better, but for a moment it seemed the fog was escaping into the plane like the mist that had covered the actor in the 1957 movie *The Incredible Shrinking Man*.

"Jerks," said Sid Packer, a middle-aged salesman. The words burst out from his first-class window seat next to Blake Stone, the soul unfortunate enough to be Packer's seatmate.

"We're going back to Atlanta, I just know it." Packer was upset at the flight attendant, the pilot, and the airline, not to mention the weather. "I have an important meeting tomorrow morning in Dallas, and they're going to cost me plenty."

Just then the pilot came on, interrupting Packer's string of complaints with reality, telling his passengers they would be circling and would do so for another thirty minutes.

If the fog didn't clear, the plane and its human payload would be heading back to Atlanta. The first leg had been late leaving Detroit due to several inches of snow, and they had barely made the connection in Atlanta. Now Birmingham and Jackson both were socked in, and it looked like Atlanta was back on the agenda.

It was a night of U-turns.

Packer was so much like others Blake had sat next to. They couldn't handle the fact they were not the center of the universe, so they had to blame someone. And more often than not, it was the flight attendants who took the brunt of their anger.

Seeking relief from Packer's badgering, Blake's attention moved without much effort to the lovely woman sitting next to him across the aisle in 2C. He was trying to decide if he should speak. She was reading, something many passengers do to pass the hours.

Now, talking among passengers is done, but there is an unwritten rule that says not to intrude if someone is sleeping or reading or working. However, it is done, but selectively. Blake had to get away from the loudmouth or he just might kill him. And he could, Blake thought. With just a quick twist of the head, and the entire cabin would do the wave. But no, Packer would live a little longer.

Blake could wait no longer and leaned into the aisle to get closer. "Hi. I'm Blake Stone."

The blond, blue-eyed woman turned to see who was interrupting her reading as Blake offered an apologetic smile.

She looked up at Blake. He suddenly realized he'd disturbed her reading. Her first look seemed indecisive, but a smile began to blossom. He felt hope.

He saw her put her slender finger in the book she was reading. He was glad she was just keeping her place. If she had grabbed the book he might've had to duck. The smile blossomed. "Hello, I'm Julie Thomas."

"Hi, Julie. I noticed you're reading *A Walk Among the Tombstones*. Do you like it?"

"Oh, yes. I like his writing."

That gave John a lead. "So do I, but I'm puzzled because that book came in 1991, no, 1992 . . . Hm, well, in there somewhere. So how did you get interested in his writing?"

"My dad. He has a lot of old books. And when I have time, I ask him for a favorite. He gave me two of Block's books, as a starter." She grinned wide. "This is the first and I like it so far."

"Well, your dad knows his books. So, what do you think of Matt and Elaine's relationship?"

The lead character, Matthew Scudder, was an ex-cop who often worked for shady characters, and Elaine was his call-girl girlfriend.

"Well, I'm just over halfway through, but I think they love each other. And he sure is *understanding* about her line of work. Most men couldn't handle it." She paused, thinking that could cross some bounds.

"I'm in cosmetics. What about you?" she asked.

"Consulting."

"Doesn't everyone. Oh, please forgive me, I meant nothing by that, but there are just so many doing consulting work."

It did not hurt Blake's feelings. "No problem, and I agree."

"What kind of consulting do you do?"

"Let's just say I help people make their problems go away."

That was as much as he wanted to share for now, and he changed the subject.

"I can see why you're in the cosmetics field. Please don't be offended, but you're very attractive."

"I'm not offended. I'm also not liberated. And thank you."

"So, how'd you get started doing that?"

"Easy. My father has a cosmetics firm." She offered a smile with those words. "I started working at his company as a secretary. As I got older, he had me moved to making appearances."

"Seems your beauty blossomed early."

"Well, that's for someone else to say. Blossomed? You do have a way with words. All I know is I've been making special appearances and doing makeup demonstrations for as long as I can remember. I've always worked for Father. He's a kind and sweet man, and if I'm helping him with his business, that makes me happy."

"I see you're not wearing a ring. Hope you don't mind my noticing that? I'd expect you'd be getting wedding proposals every day."

"That's kind for you to say, and I see you're not wearing a ring either." She grinned, but it turned into a grimace as she added, "Now, I did get one proposal, but he turned out to be a drunk and abusive, so I had to get rid of him. I can't believe I even told you that. It's not something I speak of, and I sure don't talk about it. Forgive me?"

"Nothing to forgive. I'm glad he didn't hurt you, and from what I see, nothing has. Oh, and I promise to not pass it on." And he certainly wouldn't.

"Blake, what do you think they're going to do with us?"

"There's a flight out at six. If we get back to Atlanta, say, at two and get settled, there won't be enough time to go to and return from a hotel. Won't be worth it. No, it's my bet we'll sleep at one of the gates."

At that moment, the flight attendant announced that was just what they would be doing.

"I'm impressed. You must travel a lot?" Julie smiled.

Blake was entranced by her smile. It was not the first time he'd met a woman on a plane, a meeting that extended overnight. But he shouldn't get ahead of himself.

"Just been in a lot of these situations."

"They don't care," came the abrupt statement from Sid Packer.

Blake, surprised by the noise, turned his head to Packer then quickly back again to Julie. Blake raised his eyes and shook his head slightly, letting Julie know he didn't like the interruption.

"Excuse me," he said to Julie, then turned to Packer. "They care. Besides, they want to get home, too."

"They'll do whatever they please," said Packer to Blake, to the window, whoever would listen.

Julie heard it too. So did most of the first-class cabin.

Blake had to reply. "People are getting tired of your complaining. Order a drink and shut up."

Packer looked at Blake, stunned that some stranger would talk to him that way.

Blake turned back to Julie before Packer could answer. "Sorry for the interruption."

Julie leaned over the arm of the chair as close as she could. Blake responded in like manner.

"I feel so sorry for you. You have to sit next to that jerk. What's his problem?"

Blake shrugged.

The announcement had caused a flurry of activity in both cabins. Blake saw one of the men in row four extract the airphone from its rest and make a call. That wouldn't seem so significant, except the man was looking at Blake, or at least in his direction. It was not a pleasant look.

Blake was distracted by the soft voice next to him and missed the first few words.

Julie had started talking: ". . . get a little sleep, but I'll have bags under my eyes at the demonstration bigger than my overnight case."

"I'm sure they'd be beautiful bags," quipped Blake, liking this conversation more and more.

"That's sweet," she said before being interrupted.

"Two-bit airline. They won't even put us up in a decent hotel. We'll have to sleep on the floor," came another burst from Packer. He made himself known to most all around him.

Before Blake could turn and speak, Julie spoke up, angry. "Mister, it would be stupid to go to a hotel for three hours."

"I don't care. I paid my money, and I deserve better treatment."

Blake was getting tired of this.

He looked at her with frustration covering his face. He was a stranger. She didn't know him, but that empty seat next to her looked inviting. He was fortunate she saw his frustration.

Julie wiggled her finger at Blake to come closer. He did.

"Look, this seat next to me is empty. Would you like to change?"

"I'd love to. If you really don't mind?"

Julie didn't say a word. She just unbuckled her belt and moved to 2D next to the window. That was as good a yes as he had ever received.

As Blake was sitting down, he asked, "If you'd rather have the aisle?"

"No. This is fine. I'd rather you not be beside Captain Jerk."

They shared a grin. The flight attendants darkened the cabins and started a movie. It didn't matter. Blake and Julie continued to talk.

About thirty minutes into the movie, the woman back in 5A screamed then yelled, "It's a *rat*! A *big rat* just crawled over my feet!"

With that announcement, several more screams were heard; passengers jumped to their feet, jumped into seats, stood up, or moved into the aisles in both directions, not knowing where the rat was.

Flight attendants turned on the lights looking for the rat. After a few million loud, screaming minutes, the cabin crew caught the rat and quickly placed it out of sight of the passengers, who were then reassured this would not happen again.

The passengers moved all around each other trying to get back to their seats. With everyone settled, the lights went out again and everyone settled back into the movie or sleep.

After about half an hour, Julie commented how quiet Packer had become. He was so still he must have finally gone to sleep. Blake turned around to look, but Packer didn't look right. He had let his seat back, but his face was resting against the cabin wall. He also remembered Packer had stood up for a moment then sat back down, almost ignoring the rat event.

Blake unbuckled his seat belt and moved to his old seat next to Packer, then pushed against Packer's shoulder. Nothing. He looked back at Julie with his arms in the air and an *I have no idea* look. Julie tilted her head sideways.

Blake then touched Packer's throat. No heartbeat. Blake checked his pulse. Nothing.

Julie whispered as loud as she could, "What's wrong?"

Blake was satisfied. Packer was dead. Blake moved back next to Julie.

"He's got no heartbeat and no blood flow in his neck. Packer's dead."

Julie covered her mouth as if to silence any noise that might come out.

Blake then went and told the head flight attendant, Marsha, who did her own checking and confirmed Blake's diagnosis.

Next thing, the captain appeared. They placed a blanket on the body but didn't cover the head.

Julie was taking it all in. "Why did they cover him up?"

Blake whispered, "Airlines don't like dead passengers. He looks like he's sleeping. If it were daytime, they might cover his head too, but for sure they would move passengers from around him. They also don't like their live passengers sitting next to a dead one."

"Mr. Stone?" came the captain's voice from behind. Blake turned to face the captain. "Mr. Stone, may I see you up front?" Blake nodded and followed the captain to the first-class galley area. "Marsha said you found Mr. Packer dead. Is that true?"

"Yes, well, my new seatmate, Julie, the woman sitting next to me, noticed he got quiet and looked like he was sleeping. And when I looked, he didn't look right. His face was resting against the cabin wall next to the window. It didn't look natural, so I checked."

"Are you a doctor?" asked the captain.

"No. Just someone who's seen enough deaths to know what to look for."

"I see, maybe. It was probably a heart attack. We've had them before. Not too often, of course. We'll have a doctor in Atlanta check him. Thanks for your help, Mr. Stone."

"You're welcome, captain, but it wasn't a heart attack."

With that, the captain stood straight up, puzzled. "I'm sorry . . . how do you know it wasn't?"

"When I felt for a heartbeat on the side of his neck, I felt a small, pin-size bead, and when I pulled my fingers away, it had stuck on my finger. Here." Blake pulled out a tissue and opened it up. "Put this under a light and you'll see the tiny red drop of blood. An MD can verify. Course, his and my DNA will be in the dot."

The captain took it and stared at it for a moment. "Yes . . ." But he said nothing more.

Blake continued. "I believe he was injected with something, probably while he was sleeping or while we were all excited about the rat."

The captain was bewildered. He was in the middle of a real problem if Packer had been murdered.

"Did you know Mr. Packer?" The captain was getting more curious.

"Nope. Never saw him before this flight. He was just an obnoxious passenger on flight 1444. Captain, I might also mention this. You're missing a passenger."

"I'm what?"

"There was a man sitting behind Packer when we took off, and he was there at least till the movie started. That's about the time I moved across the aisle."

"It's funny you should mention that. When we did our seat check, before takeoff, we had five more tickets than passengers."

"You're saying those people presented a ticket at the gate, but didn't get on the plane?" queried Blake.

"That would explain it."

"How many no-shows did you have in first class? And were they true first class or upgrades?"

The captain checked with the head attendant and returned with an answer of four first class, none of which were upgrades. And one in coach.

"Is that unusual?"

"A little. This is a 757. We have twenty-four first-class seats. With five no-shows, that's more than normal, but it can happen."

"You can tell the passengers what you want, but I would have a doctor *and* the police waiting for us in Atlanta. And I would suggest you not let anyone off the plane until they confirm the cause of death. Don't let anything off the plane. One other thing. Don't let them clean the restrooms, and don't let them empty the waste tanks."

The captain left, puzzled.

Blake returned to his seat and explained his theory to Julie. He made sure she would act as if everything were okay. It might mean nothing, for the killer had surely seen Blake check on Packer.

And after the tête-à-tête with the captain, if there was a killer, he knew the captain and Blake at least had their suspicions.

As Blake turned the facts over in his mind, he knew it was possible, but not easy, to smuggle a gun onto a plane. It was very possible to smuggle the parts of a homemade weapon, parts that didn't look like barrels and triggers. He'd proved that could be done. But silencing it was next to impossible from only a few feet away.

Besides, he had taken a quick look at the seat behind Packer and hadn't seen any holes or punctures, and there was no blood on Packer except the small bead on his neck.

The other question was, Why had someone bought a ticket, come to the gate, presented the ticket to the attendant at the door to the jetway, and not boarded the plane? And why were there so many first-class no-shows?

"Why did you tell him not to empty the waste tanks?"

"Without opening a door, which is not advisable at thirty thousand feet, there is no way to get anything off the plane. A plane must be kept pressurized based on the altitude, which means it's sealed tight. You can't open a window and toss out your weapon. But if your weapon is small enough, it can be flushed down the toilet and into the waste tanks. And as soon as a plane hits the gate, they empty the tank, so if you flushed your weapon, it would soon be gone, never to be recovered."

"I would never have thought of that."

Blake had. He'd seen it.

The plane landed and pulled up to its parking place. Police officers politely entered, accompanied by the ME and two assistants who then began examining the body. The passengers had only been told they could not leave for a few minutes. No mention of a corpse, yet.

The ME recorded his findings quickly. Julie and Blake watched his assistants take pictures of the seat area, take fingerprints, and get Packer off the plane.

The captain approached Blake again with a pair of investigators.

"Mr. Stone," said the captain, "this is Lieutenant Randall and Officer Dobbs. They are with the airport police and are investigating Packer's death." -

Randall didn't give the captain time to explain further. Blake reached up and shook the extended hand.

"May I have a few words with you up front, Mr. Stone?"

That request was pretty cut and dry. Blake rose from 2C and walked between the lieutenant and Officer Dobbs until they reached the jetway just outside the 757's main entrance. The captain joined them. The winter wind slipped between the plane and the jetway's rubber insulation cupped around the door.

Lieutenant Randall started, "I understand you were the first to find Mr. Packer dead?"

"Yes. That's true."

"And why did you suspect he was dead?"

Blake went through the same spiel as he had for the captain. The captain nodded agreement with what Blake said.

"Mr. Stone, we find a few things strange. You find a man dead, the same man you were sitting next to for most of the flight. And you also discover the bead of blood and notice missing passengers," stated Randall, pausing for a reply.

Blake took it. "Just lucky, I guess. That is, if your question were to be, 'How did I manage all this?' "

"Maybe, but we also find it strange that you don't turn up on any FBI files, IRS records, nothing. Mr. Stone, you don't seem to exist. Now, how do you explain that?"

Blake tapped his forehead and pinched his arm. "No. I'm real. I can vouch for it."

"Don't be a smart—I want some answers, and I think you have them."

"Lieutenant, I'm not trying to be uncooperative, but you're questioning the wrong man. The man, or woman, who killed Packer is still on that plane, hiding among one-hundred-twenty-plus others. I'm on your side and may be able to offer some help."

"I don't need your help, and I'll lead this investigation my way—"

Blake didn't let him finish. "Packer was poisoned, wasn't he?" He didn't give the lieutenant time to answer. "Something that acts fast, probably calms the victim or paralyzes the muscles. We've been sitting on the plane for nearly two hours while your lab did its work. You know what it was, don't you?"

Blake waited for an answer.

Randall looked at the officer, then the captain, and decided to share their findings. "Yes, he was poisoned with curare. We found a small needle prick on his neck."

Randall was frustrated. Finding a small needle among the passengers would be nearly impossible. If it was a needle, it could easily be pressed into any part of a seat. It would never be found.

"I thought that a possibility. Lieutenant, if I might suggest: someone was sitting behind Packer for the better part of the trip. That person, a man, I believe, moved from that seat to another about the time they started the movie. You and I both know that curare acts quickly, so he or she must have did him, possibly held him down or distracted him in some way, then moved away. Someone must have seen the killer move. Someone had a new seatmate just about that time during the movie, while we were distracted by the rat."

Randal was not happy. "Mr. Stone, I'm running this investigation. You will sit here and keep to yourself." He left.

Blake looked at Julie. "I gotta make a phone call while I still have a phone." Julie nodded.

Blake called his boss, Mr. Johnson.

"It's Blake. You got any word on the murder on the Atlanta Delta flight? Yeah, 1444, that's the one, and I'm deep into it and need your help. Yeah. There's a Lieutenant Randall with airport PD who's heading the investigation, and right now I'm his prime suspect. True, but he will not listen. Right? Yes. Still on the plane. Probably. Yes, that's what I think. He wouldn't know that, right? Yeah. Okay. Thanks."

Blake turned to Julie.

"Blake, you're scaring me."

"Listen. The killer is still on the plane. He has seen me and Marsha talking over the body. He's seen me talking to the captain and you. I've put you in danger."

Blake motioned for the captain. The captain came and squatted in front of Blake.

"Captain, I'm about to tell you something, and no matter what I say, do not look away from me. Focus on me and Julie. Just nod if you understand." The captain nodded, eyes on Blake.

"We know the killer is still on the plane and now must be seated farther back. Probably in a row by himself. In the dark with the movie playing and after he pricked Packer, he had to get away from the crime scene. I suggest you get

Marsha and one of the flight attendants who have been working the back areas to come up front. Not here, but in the forward attendant area, and ask them if they noticed anyone suddenly showing up in a row that was empty."

"That's going to look suspicious to the killer," said the captain.

"True. So they must appear to be doing their usual rounds. Do not let them look around. Keep them focused on you. Have them calmly walk back down the aisle comforting passengers and at the same time look for the person who wasn't there when we took off. Have them quietly and separately come back to the front, as if needed, and report what they see. Now smile, say thanks, and do that. Please?"

The captain smiled at Blake, said he liked he plan, stood up, and did what he asked.

Blake turned to Julie.

"The lieutenant will probably keep me on the plane. In any case, whatever you are told by the lieutenant, do not leave the plane with any passengers. And once in the airport, never be left alone with a passenger. Understand?"

Tears were forming in Julie's eyes. Blake held her hands and gave her comforting words. She hugged him. He hugged her and told her she was going to be okay. If there were a target, it was him.

"I'm not leaving this plane without you right by me. The lieutenant can go take a hike."

"I like that, and I'll make sure that happens."

The attendants did their looking, came back separately as instructed, and gave their info to the captain, who motioned for Blake to come join the group.

The captain introduced Blake to Betty.

"Mr. Stone, Betty has been working the back thirty-plus rows since boarding. And all the seats were occupied as they were at the start of the flight. There was no man alone in any rows."

Blake was puzzled, then had a thought.

"Betty, was there a woman in a row by herself?" Betty nodded. "Was she there when we started to take off?"

Betty said, "No, she wasn't. I remember now. That row was empty when I checked, and all three seats were to have passengers."

"Captain, that's your killer."

"Blake, you said it was a man."

"One would think so. Betty? Marsha? Do either of you know the names of the passengers who would have been in that row and in 3A?"

The two checked and came back.

Betty started, "Kelly Smith was in 3A, and Kelli Smith was in 28F, and both checked in at the counter and went through boarding. He had too. I mean she. I mean, I don't know what I mean."

Blake now had the clue. "The man I saw turned into a woman, or back into a woman. No matter how you spell the name, Kelly sounds like Kelli, and even at a glance looks the same. I suspect you will find some men's garb under his women's outerwear, and maybe even a wig flushed down the toilet. I suspect he—or is it she?— bought the extra tickets to be sure no one would be in the rows he needed."

The lieutenant suddenly made his presence known.

"Mr. Stone, I don't know who or what you are, but my manager got a call from the FBI director and was told to back off. But I'm going to ignore that and take you in anyway."

The captain announced himself. "Lieutenant, Mr. Stone is not going anywhere. By the way, he just solved your case for you."

It took some explaining, but the lieutenant and his team arrested the perpetrator, and the passengers disembarked safely. Everyone was smiling, except the lieutenant.

Blake collected Julie, including her luggage, and with the help of a private jet, courtesy of Mr. Johnson, they headed to Dallas for her appointment. They were the only two passengers and were sitting in adjoining seats with no armrest in between.

"Julie, I think you heard the lieutenant question my name?"

"Yes, but I didn't want to pry."

"My real name is Jake Stone, and I do try to help people get rid of problems."

With that, Julie cuddled up to him, laying her head on his shoulder with her arms around his. Yawning, she mumbled quietly, "I think the lieutenant finally figured out how much you helped. You knowing that Packer was in the Witness Protection Program blew his mind. Mine, too, but nothing surprises me about you. I'll have to meet Mr. Johnson some time. He seems to care about you. And the captain sure appreciated you with first class for life." Another yawn. "I was really scared at first, but you gave me hope that all would turn out right."

Her voice was getting lower . . .

"I like Jake Stone . . . and his name." And she drifted off into dreamland.

A Comforting End

Indian Summer
with Becky J. Smith

Read this first, please. When I was the newsletter editor with the Mississippi Writers Association, there was a contest to see who could write a story in one hundred words or less. We decided to make the story a total of two hundred words. Two ladies combined their talent with words and imagination to make this a winner: two parts one hundred words each, with two winners. Barbara Garrett won the first half of the story with her one hundred words, and Becky won the second half with hers. But there is a problem.

I haven't been able to find Barbara Garrett, so I can't use her hundred words. So, I wrote the first part you see below, which is different than Barbara's. Hers was great and I wish I could use it.

Why my car would break down here was bad enough. Maybe I took a wrong turn. And my cell phone couldn't get a signal in this desolate place.

"Susan, come back here! I can't go running after you with the baby."

My eldest ran after Susan, who was running full blast into the woods. My baby needed feeding, but I couldn't do that here. *Do I go back? Do I go forward?* Then I heard Susan scream, "Mama! A bear!"

The kids were running, crying and screaming, out of the woods with the bear close behind, mouth open, teeth showing.

I pulled the kids into the car and shut the door as the bear leaped—

"Cut," said Ron the director. "Bring in the mechanical bear for the next scene while we break for lunch."

"Would someone get this screaming brat off my back?" said Julia.

The assistant moved quickly to save the baby from the real terror on set: Julia Wayne, movie star.

"Ron, let's talk. I'll not be upstaged by those boring children or that infernal bear in the attack scene. If my fans only knew what I endure on location."

Smiling, Ron thought, *Another day in Hollywood.*

THE END

Book Writer

"What are you doing, Kathy? You're not supposed to be rummaging through someone's trash."

"Harry, this guy's writing a book."

"How do you know that? You're just a crazy female."

"Thanks. I'll remember that remark."

"Nobody reads books anymore. That's what I meant with crazy."

"I do! And I like his story. It's a romantic mystery."

"Romantic, shmomantic. Just don't let the boss catch you. We're supposed to be picking up trash, not reading it. Remember!"

"Remind me to give you a hug."

"I just called you crazy but didn't mean it, and you want to give me a hug?"

"Harry, if it weren't for your patience and help, I wouldn't have this job."

"Ah, now, don't go getting all mushy. You're doing a good job. And I ain't gonna tell nobody."

She gave him a hug anyway.

Katherine was a twenty-three-year-old, brown-eyed brunette working the only job she could find while trying to work her way through night school.

"My mom was worried about me doing this job with a bunch of men. I told her you were a really nice guy."

"Young lady, if you think I'm gonna cry, you got another thing coming."

"Harry, I don't expect a macho guy like you to cry. I just wanted you to know I enjoy reading and that you're a sweet guy who has stood up for me in the shop when a couple of the guys started, well, you know. I got scared and you made me feel better. You helped give me a chance."

"Ah, I was just looking after a young girl who needed looking after. And, well, okay, I'm catching up with ya. Takes a little time for an old codger like me, you know. So, how did you know he was a writer?"

"This is so exciting. It was last month. A sheet fell out of his trash, and I was about to toss it back when I saw it was a page out of a story. Since then, I've been rummaging through his trash. I kept looking and finding more."

"Now, why didn't I notice this rummaging?"

"Well, the guy doesn't have much trash. He either doesn't throw anything away or doesn't have anything *to* throw away. So after we got his stuff, I kept his bag out, looked through, and tossed it in the crusher at the next stop."

"You mean you've been doing all that hanging on the back of this rig?"

"Yes, sir."

"Girl, now I know you're crazy."

"Guess I am. But when I saw the pages made a story, I couldn't stop looking. Harry, the more pages I found, the more the story came to life."

"We been working together for a couple of months now, and you're a nice girl. And I really didn't mean that crazy talk. I'm just an old guy, and Kathy, if I had a girl I'd want her to be just like you."

"Harry, that's so sweet. And I might like that, too. Some of the guys told me your wife died a long time ago. I was sorry to hear that. My dad died when I was fifteen. He loved to read, and it flowed over to me."

"I didn't know that. Is your mother okay?"

"Oh, yes. She's great. She can't work much, so I have to do this to help pay the bills."

"I see. Well, you keep collecting his papers, but you will do it *inside* the cab. With me, understand?"

"Okay, Pop," she said with a playful grin.

"Ah, jeez, don't say that . . ." Then he paused, looking at her. "You know, I mean, I guess . . . well, it's okay if you want to call me Pop. Anytime you want to."

"It's a deal, Pop. And I do mean that."

They finished their rounds smiling and laughing about all kinds of trash.

Another week and today was the day. After work, Kathy cleaned up and dressed in blue jeans and a blouse her dad had given her for her birthday—the last birthday she'd celebrated with him. It was a special day, and the blouse made it extra special.

Approaching the guy's house with the torn, mangled, and dirty pages she had collected snuggled in her arms, Kathy reminded herself that she had to meet this man.

Katherine rang the doorbell. No one came to the door. She pressed the doorbell again. No one. Discouraged, she held her pages close to her and turned to leave.

Then she heard, "Can I help you?"

Excited, she spun around and saw a nice-looking young man holding the door open. He was wearing a blue shirt that needed an iron and glasses held together over his nose with a piece of tape. She almost laughed when she saw him, but she was so happy he'd opened the door that it didn't matter for now.

She replied, "Yes. My name is Katherine. I've been reading your book and I love it."

"You what? My book's not published. It's not finished yet. How—"

She interrupted him. "Please forgive me. I'm just so excited to meet you. And I guess I owe you an apology and an explanation. Please let me come in, or maybe we can talk here on the porch?"

The man looked puzzled. She saw him looking around and behind her. The only other person visible was a man across the street cutting his grass. She could tell he was trying to decide.

"I may be foolish, but come in. You don't look dangerous. And if you had a gun, you couldn't hide it under what you're wearing." He stopped and his face turned red. "I'm so sorry for being so forward. Please come in."

Katherine walked into his house, giving him a smile as she passed him. But when she was fully inside, it was obvious he lived alone. No woman would leave it looking as she saw it.

She turned to face him. "I'm Katherine Walker. Thank you for seeing me. Oh, and your name is Elijah Rivers."

"My name's William MacBride. How did you know my pen name?"

Katherine left him guessing. "May I sit down?"

William pointed at the sofa, then sat down in a nearby chair.

Katherine started, "Now, this is going to sound really strange. It does even to me. I collect your garbage on Tuesdays and Fridays. And one—"

"I don't believe you. You're a beautiful woman. A young, beautiful woman. You collect garbage?"

"Thank you, and you're a nice-looking guy. And I do collect your garbage. I told you my story would seem strange and maybe unbelievable. Please listen. Last month, as I was emptying your garbage can, a sheet of paper fell out. I was about to throw it in the truck when I noticed it was a page of a story."

He started to speak, but she shushed him.

"I read the page and loved it. I quickly looked and found more pages. I grabbed them all, tucked them into my shirt, and finished my route. When I got home, I cleaned them and put them in order. I was making your book. I've been doing that ever since. I don't have all the pages, but I love the ones I have. Mr. MacBride, you are a wonderful storyteller."

She then held out the soiled, wrinkled pages for him to see.

He took the pages, sat quietly, and started looking at them, amazed by what he had heard and what he was holding. And all was coming from such a lovely woman.

"Miss Katherine, you're a garbage collector? How can that be?"

"Just Kathy is fine. I need the money. It's just Mom and me, and the job was available and gave me time off to do classes. May I call you William?"

"Please do. Most call me Mac. You can call me anything you want." Katherine offered him a smile. He smiled back. This was so unexpected William did not know what to do next.

Katherine saw his confusion. "I like William. It sounds royal." She had been looking at his feet and just had to know. "Forgive me for asking, but you're barefooted. Do you have any shoes?'

"Oh, yes. But one of them has a hole in it. I need to get it fixed."

She became suspicious. "How long has that hole been there?"

"I don't really remember. I noticed it back in December when my sock got wet."

"December was six months ago. At least we know you have socks. But we'll worry about that later. You wouldn't happen to have any iced tea or hot tea or water?"

"Well, ah, no. I had some instant coffee this morning. I don't cook too well. I do have some hot tea bags my mother left."

Katherine was ready. "Perfect. I'll make us some tea. Do you drink hot tea?"

"Yes. I'm just not good at making it."

She thought to herself, *All you have to do is heat water and drop a bag in it.* "I'll make us some. Do you cook at all?"

"No. I just go to fast-food places and—"

"Is that all you eat? Fast food?"

"Pretty much, unless Mom comes over."

"Where does your mom live?"

"Rome."

"I assume that's Georgia. And that's on the other side of the state, hours away. Okay. It's just about lunchtime. When's the last time you ate? Did you eat breakfast?"

"Yeah, it's Georgia. I had a donut and coffee."

"Sweetie, I'm fixing you lunch. A real lunch."

William mumbled an okay as he watched her head for the kitchen. She wasn't gone long. "When's the last time you bought groceries?"

"I don't remember."

"Neither does your pantry. It looks like you just moved in. The pantry is starving. Give me some money. I'll go buy you some food, and it looks like I better plan on fixing it— often."

Katherine held out her hand.

William opened his wallet and gave her a hundred dollars, without question.

"Go work on your book. I'll be back within an hour."

He gave her an okay.

She gave him a kiss . . . the first of many, along with a lot of meals, a lot of encouragement, and the love a woman gives her husband.

They published a lot of novels together over the years.

As to Harry, well, she kept on calling him Pop. Now, maybe the relationship wasn't biological, but he got the daughter he always wanted and she got a new father.

Harry escorted Kathy down the aisle at her wedding.

A Novel End

Jive Talking in the Twenty-First Century

It was early morning, just a quarter to nine. Jeeves, the butler, entered the bedroom with a message: "Ms. Judy, you received an e-mail from Mr. Robby regarding dinner tonight at La Augare."

"Jeeves, reply back that Mother will be here and we'll have to postpone till next week."

"Yes, ma'am. I will do that." He left the room.

On her phone, she texted, *Robby, Mother coming today. We planned last week.*

Robby texted back, *I forgot.*

After only a few minutes, Jeeves returned. "Mr. Robby wants to know if he can bring some friends from the office for a card game Saturday."

"E-mail him back saying it's okay, but be sure to make it in the afternoon. Maybe twoish."

"Yes, ma'am," said Jeeves, leaving the room.

Robby texted, *Judy, let's plan trip to Spain this year. Just the two of us.*

She texted back, *Love the idea. Let's do that.*

Robby's reply: *I'll get the plans started.*

Jeeves returned again. Standing at the foot of the bed, he said, "Mr. Robby is asking me to check on Spain . . ." Then he boldly said, "ENOUGH! Will you two stop this? E-mails and texting, and you're lying there next to each other. For God's sake, your shoulders are touching. Why don't you just talk? *Please?*"

"Sorry, Jeeves," said Robby.

"Yeah. Me too," said Judy. Judy turned to the left. "Maybe we should get up, sweetheart?"

"Would you text me on that, Judy?"

Jeeves replied, rolling his eyes. "I'll get you both some clothes." He went into the closet and slammed the door.

Fini

A Bed of Roses

"Must you go to the office today? It's Saturday. I thought we'd spend some time together," said Kitty.

She and Tom had been married for twelve years.

Tom put his arms around her. "Not today, sweet. Winslow from corporate is coming in on Monday, and I have some reports to finish. It'll be my head if I don't get them done. While I'm gone, you can work on your roses. They're looking very special."

Kitty had been tending her rose garden for three years, getting it ready for the horticultural committee. She was trying to win first place. Tom had cleared the garden area himself and had had the greenhouse built for her when he had first started his business travels, over three years ago.

"Okay. I understand. Well, I do understand, but I don't like it. Please don't stay too late, okay?"

"I'll be home by four."

With that, Tom gave her a hug and a kiss and left. Kitty changed her clothes and went into the greenhouse.

Kitty didn't like the late nights during the week and the Saturday work that had been happening for a long time.

She knew she and Tom loved each other, but she also knew they had both been putting other *things* ahead of themselves as a couple.

Kitty was replanting a Mr. Lincoln that was sick when Peggy appeared at the greenhouse door. Kitty motioned for Peggy to come in.

"You better be glad the windows in here are translucent, or your neighbors would be having a fit. Well, the women would. The men would be buying new, high-powered binoculars or sneaking a peek through the cracks," quipped Peggy.

Peggy knew that Kitty wore a bikini in the greenhouse and slipped into overalls, covering her bikini, when she went into the garden. They had been friends since the high-school cheerleading team, and Peggy knew better than anyone how her friend dressed. She just liked to tease a bit.

"If anybody could see in, I wouldn't do it. If you spent as much time in this hothouse as I do, you'd be tossing off your clothes, too," replied Kitty.

"I . . . don't think so. Besides, the men would buy *blindfolds* if I did it."

"Now, that's not true and you know it."

Grinning, Peggy said, "Still, you're going to get caught one of these days. What does Tom think of your garden-variety bikini?"

That was all it took. Kitty got quiet then started crying.

Peggy moved closer and attempted to console her. After the tears slowed, she said, "Okay, girl. What's going on?" Peggy asked.

"Let's go inside. All of a sudden, I want to get some clothes on."

Once inside, Kitty changed then joined Peggy in the kitchen, who had started a pot of hot tea.

"I don't know what to do," Kitty said, pouring them each a cup. "For the longest time, Tom has spent more time at the office than at home. We haven't made love in two months. I don't know what's wrong. I've still got my figure. I'm a pretty good cook. I just don't know."

This gave Peggy the opportunity she wanted, had wanted, for weeks. "I knew something wasn't right. You don't see it, do you?"

"See what?"

"When I got here today, where were you?"

"In the greenhouse."

"When I called you yesterday afternoon, where were you?"

"In my . . ." She didn't finish.

"And where are you every day, and Saturdays, and Sundays, and evenings?"

"I know where you're heading, but my garden is my hobby. Besides, I don't spend that much time working in it."

Kitty knew she hadn't, at first, and it had all started innocently. Tom had begun traveling a great deal and had continued to play golf most Saturdays. All that had caused her to start her own hobby. Tom had even suggested she start a hobby because of all his trips, and it had looked like they were going to continue. She had thought it would keep her from feeling lonely.

But his traveling had stopped.

Petty knew. "Oh, yes, you do. Think about it. Count the hours."

Kitty sat quietly. The steam from her cup grew smaller.

"Oh. Dear God. You're right. Ever since I increased my effort to win that contest, he's been . . . he's had no reason to be at home. I'm always out there. When I first started, I wore regular work clothes. Then he built the greenhouse for me. I don't even know if he knows I wear," the words were straining to come out, "my bikini in the greenhouse," said Kitty as her eyes began to water.

"He may not know about the bikini, but you know this. The man loves you. You two once did everything together."

"You're right. I pushed him away from me. He tried many times to do things with me, but I always had a reason not to." She pointed toward the garden.

Betty, the receptionist, had stopped by to pick up something, and as she made a pass by Tom's desk she stopped. He was staring at his computer. She saw an untouched cup of coffee had turned cold, and the screen saver on his PC was saving away.

"You look like you lost your best friend," said Betty.

Startled, his head jumped to attention. Looking up at her, he said, "Oh! Hi Betty." Then, more calmly, he added, "If I didn't know better, I'd think she didn't love me anymore."

Betty only knew Kitty from the office parties, but Tom played golf with her husband, Scott.

"I assume you mean your wife?"

Tom gave her an *Of course I do* look.

Betty put her package down on his desk. "Last I heard, mostly from you, you'd stake your life on it. Something change?"

"No. Not really, but she spends so much time in her garden."

"You told me she was trying to win a prize, right?" asked Betty.

"Yes."

"And didn't you build that greenhouse for her?"

"Sure. She needed that. It was important to her."

Betty slowly said, "As I recall, before the garden, you two went on all kinds of trips. And I'll bet she did all the work planning and getting ready."

"Yes, she had more time than me."

"And she washed your clothes, ironed your shirts, pressed your pants, cooked your meals, right?" asked Betty.

"Well, yes. Sure, but—"

"Before the travel, you played golf with Scott. And didn't you keep playing golf on Saturdays with Scott while you were traveling two and three weeks of each month?"

"Okay. Okay. Okay. I hear you. She did all that for me, and I rewarded her by abandoning her on Saturdays. Now she has a hobby, and I don't like it."

"Bingo," Betty added as she snapped her fingers.

"I'm a real jerk."

"No, you're not a jerk. Well, maybe a small, lovable one. You love her. She loves you. I suggest you show it."

Tom knew what she said was right. He needed to do something special for Kitty. He decided to buy her a special rose to show his support, and it would be something that might help her win first prize. At the fourth nursery he visited, he found a new hybrid peach rose and bought it. He couldn't pronounce the name, but it was special.

As he parked the car, he went around back. He figured she would be in the garden. But he couldn't believe his eyes. Someone had stripped the petals off the rose bushes. There was nothing left but stems.

Frightened and afraid something had happened to Kitty, he ran into the house calling her name. The thought of calling 911 raced through his mind, but he didn't want to take the time in case she needed him now.

When he reached the foyer, he saw a stream of rose petals littering the stairs. At first, he moved cautiously up the stairs, but after two steps he couldn't hold his feelings at bay. He took the rest of the steps two and three at a time following the flow.

The rose petals stopped at their bedroom door. He approached it carefully, afraid of what lay behind it. He turned the knob and pushed the door open.

Standing in the doorway, rose plant in hand, his eyes fell upon the most beautiful sight he had ever seen.

The trail of rose petals led to their bed. Kitty was lying on their bed, wearing only a bikini. She was holding a single rose.

"Kitty, I brought you this . . . rose . . . hybrid . . . thing" was all he could muster.

Kitty rose up on one elbow and wiggled her finger for him to join her.

Tom moved to her side.

"You didn't have to do this."

"Yes, darling, I did have to do this. Now, put the plant over there and," she patted the bed beside her, "plant yourself right here."

A Rosy End

Denver Passage

I was walking through the hotel lobby when I suddenly felt faint and began to wobble from side to side. If you've ever been to Denver, then you know. It's the altitude. Denver isn't called the Mile-High City for nothing. After I composed myself and looked around to see if anyone had seen me wobble, I flagged the valet to get my car. I had arrived last night, and this was my day to see the Rockies. The city of Boulder showed up, and I bought gas, got a snack, and visited the men's room. From there it was up Highway 6 to Rolling Fork.

I was doing pretty good managing the twisting, turning curves, till I had to swerve to miss a rather large rock the stone-faced wall had released. The back wheel caught the rock, causing the rear end to leap from the pavement and drop down hard. That's when I heard another thump and a small "Ouch!" from the trunk.

"Ouch?" I had heard it. This was a rental, and I knew I hadn't paid for one that spoke.

I pulled the car over and drew my .45 from the glove compartment, then got out of the car. I figured I could open it or head for a police station. I'm the "take a chance" type. I held my gun behind me, turned the key, moved to one side, and quickly flipped up the trunk lid.

This time it was a short, female scream. She lay there curled up in a fetal position. She was barefooted and wearing scanty pajamas. Her arms were across her chest as if protecting herself, eyes wide open and nearing tears. Her blond hair lay mostly behind her head with some loose strands across her face.

She appeared harmless. I slipped my weapon behind my belt so she wouldn't see it and would hopefully calm down some.

"Look, I don't know who you are or what you're doing in my trunk, but you look very uncomfortable. Would you like to get out? Actually, I'd like for you to. Please? Oh, and my name is David."

She continued to look up at me. It was my time again. I backed away several feet. "You have my word. I won't harm you. Really, I won't. This is pretty unusual for me. I've never found a girl, well, where you are. Please?"

After an eternity, she raised herself up and literally crawled out, never taking her eyes off me. Once out, she moved to the side of the car . . . and stood there.

I moved back another few feet and sat down on the ground to show I meant her no harm. I figured it was time for an introduction.

"My name is David Jansen. I'm twenty-six, not married and I live in Cartersville, Georgia. I was seeing some clients in St. Louis and Denver. While here, I decided to see the Rockies close up. And then you appeared in my trunk. I must admit, I've had many things in there, but never anything as pretty as you. Please tell me about yourself, why you hid in my car, and what I can do to help you."

She walked slowly to the back bumper and sat down cross legged on the grass.

"My name is Nancy Wagner. I'm nineteen and . . ." She paused there, to gather her thoughts, I guess. "And some men are after me. I got away from them and was hiding. When you left your car back in Boulder, I looked, and it was unlocked and the keys were in it. I opened the truck, got in, and closed the lid."

She stopped. I figured it was my time.

"Funny, but I never leave my keys in the car. Why I did this time, I have no idea. Why are these men after you?'

"They kidnapped me."

I didn't expect that. "Do your parents know? You can use my phone to call them."

"I don't have any parents. They died last year."

"I'm so sorry, Nancy. Do you have anyone we can call?"

"I have a couple of friends, but without my phone I don't have their numbers. Besides, they're in Georgia."

I'm sure both you and I are noticing just how puzzling this was. Usually people kidnap someone and ask for money.

"But why did they kidnap you? If there is no one to pay the ransom, why would they?"

Maybe the question scared her, because she still looked very afraid. And she didn't know me. Why should she answer me? But I hoped she would.

Then came her answer. "I can't tell you."

Hm, guess I'm not the right type. I figured I should try someone with a uniform.

"Nancy, I know you don't know me, but I don't want those men to find you either. If you will let me, I'll take you to the Denver police. They will—"

"NO. No." Her hands covered her face and she started to cry.

Decision time. Would she let me take her to Denver, or for that matter, anywhere? The situation was perplexing. For anything to occur, I had to get her to confide in me the real problem. Her question seemed to be just how much she could trust me. Or how trustworthy I was. She had no weapon. That was obvious because all she had on was the pajamas. The top was tight and the bottoms were short, very short. Only the natural bulges were showing. Even a toothpick would announce itself.

"Nancy, we can sit here all day and night and get nowhere. I don't know if I can trust you. You don't trust me, and I can understand that. I can't believe what I'm about to do. Look, if you will get in the car, I'll take you anywhere you want to go. And I mean anywhere."

I waited for a response. Silence.

"Okay, well, I'll let you have my car, and you go wherever you want to go, just promise to send someone to come get me. I'll give you my keys and walk a long way off so you can leave easily. I must be stupid and crazy, but I'll do it."

I made a mental note to have my head examined, and pulled several twenties from my wallet and the car keys out of my pocket. I put the twenties on the ground and laid the keys on top of the money.

As I stood up, she did so as well. I started walking to the driver side. She moved to the passenger side. I retrieved my briefcase and small bag. I turned to look at her over the roof for a moment, then crossed the road and started walking up the road, thinking, *I'm a real, stupid, dumb dummy.*

But she needed to trust someone, and maybe it was me.

Taking a slow, slight glance back, she was standing there watching me walk away. Looked like I'd have to call a taxi.

After a short time and a couple car lengths up the road, Nancy yelled, "Yes. You are crazy. What're you doing?"

Turning to face her, I shouted back, "I'm leaving my car. I don't know all that's going on, but you need to trust someone. I'm available, but I'm not going to force you. Please send someone to get me."

I turned and continued to walk . . . hoping.

From behind me, I heard the door shut, the car start, then wheels spinning and screeching as the rubber hit the road. *Oh shit, she's going to run me down!* I turned in time to see her pull up beside me. She slammed on the brakes and I heard the car going into park. She got out and walked around to the passenger side.

She opened the door. "Get in. You're driving." It was time to take orders.

I watched her for a few seconds. Her lips were somewhere in between a smile and a grimace. The moment seemed to be in my court.

"If it's all right with you, I'd really like to go back to Denver. It's a very long way over the Rockies to civilization."

More pleasant waiting. Finally, she said okay and got in. Joining her, I turned the car around and again saw her pretty, bare feet.

"First thing we gotta do is get you some shoes. Okay?"

She said yes again, this time with a small smile.

"Your feet must hurt. There're lots of small rocks along here. Do they hurt?"

In a low voice she said, "Yes."

"Thought so. Don't worry. I'll take care of that. I saw a discount store on Hampden. You will need a bit more than shoes. We'll start there. If we can't find all you need there, we'll find a clothing store."

From the time Nancy got in the car, she never took her eyes off me. She was either trying to read my mind, or drill holes in my head, or who knows what. She said okay. There was something under her nails, so I gave her a tissue and asked her to clean them. It's rare to see a woman with dirty nails. Us guys, well, that's a different story. She finished and returned the tissue with a soft thank-you.

Nancy was quiet for a while. As we approached Boulder, I had her slide down in the seat to avoid being seen. Her abductors must be looking for her. We drove on through Boulder. As we got a few miles out, I saw no one following us, so we headed for Denver.

Then right out of the blue, she asked, "David, why are you doing all this? You don't even know . . ." And she stopped.

I was wondering myself. She was beautiful and helpless. Guess that stuck in my male mind. "You know, if you would tell me what all this is about, I might could help. I won't get any police involved. I'm an investigator. You can call me a detective, meaning I just may be able to help you."

"You mean a private detective like Philip Marlowe?" Her smile grew a little when she said that. Cool. Making progress.

"And who played the best Marlowe?"

"Why, Bogart, of course."

"Not many people your age would know that. I'm impressed."

"My dad liked old movies, and I watched them with him. I got to liking them, too."

"Nancy, I truly want to help you. Until you want to tell me what's going on, I can at least buy you clothes and take you wherever you want to go. If that's all you'll let me do, then that's all. I want to do more. Don't ask me why. I look at you and can't do anything but want to help."

"David, I've known you about half an hour and I already see that you are a kind person. And I have a feeling you have a great respect for women and want to make sure a woman is safe. You proved you're a sweet man. I feel that, too."

"Thank you. I appreciate your nice words. And I want to help any way I can."

She continued. "When my parents died, they left me money. Those men want that money. My dad had a lawyer he used for years. I continued to use him, and suddenly realized he was cheating me. Stealing. And, I suspect, he was cheating my dad as well. I called him on it and fired him. He threatened me. I ignored him, and two nights ago two guys broke into my house and took me. They put something over my face, and the next thing I remember, I'm in Boulder. They left me in the car. Guess they figured I was still drugged. But I woke up and hid in your car."

"I'm glad I left the keys in it."

"Me too."

I shook my head. "Those men still want you. We need to get off this road. I don't want to pass them and risk them seeing you. We're probably lucky already. I'm not going back through Denver. We're heading south. Maybe we should go through Colorado Springs and home from there. How does that sound?"

"Sounds good. Yes. Please. Thank you."

I was making progress. "Are you hungry?"

"Yes. Very."

I pressed buttons on the GPS, looking for a place to eat other than Denver, and found a nearby small town off the main track between Boulder and Denver.

"Next road is Boulder Road. It will take us to Lafayette. Not far. Under an hour. We can eat there. Oh, and get you some clothes, and hope I don't get arrested for what you are wearing."

"I'm so ashamed for not telling you about all this. I'm causing you so much trouble."

"You're not causing me any trouble. I must admit, I'm enjoying your company. And you have nothing to be ashamed of. You could trust no one. Nancy, I think you're smart and brave. I bet the only time you were afraid was when they grabbed you and put halothane or—hopefully not—chloroform over your face. There are other drugs they could have used. At least they haven't harmed you."

"How did . . . have you investigated something like this before? You have, haven't you?"

"Mr. Harper told me I could read people pretty quick. I don't know."

"Who's Mr. Harper?"

"He was an investigator. He found me and brought me in under his wing. He died a couple years ago, but he taught me a lot. He had no children, so it seems I was it. He was a great teacher. Guess you'd say he was my second father. Mom's still alive and lives near me in Cartersville. My dad died when I was sixteen, much like your father. We just weren't rich."

"I like your story. It has much love in it."

"He was a super guy. We had lots of experiences and fun, too. Forgive me, one thing I don't understand. You were taken in Georgia and ended up in Boulder heading I don't know where. Please explain."

"Oh, David. There's so much. Be prepared for more truth."

"You can tell me when you get ready. When you want to."

"Now's the time. Daddy had manufacturing plants in Denver and Oklahoma. My older brother runs them and has an interest in all Dad's property. When Daddy died, his will gave it all to me. All of it. I've not been close to my brother—ever. I came along nine years after him. Seems I was an accident."

Nodding, I responded, "I've heard of similar families myself. But they usually stay close even with the many years between siblings."

"Maybe it was the wealth and power. I don't know. He quickly moved up in Dad's businesses when I was young and a nobody. When my brother was beginning to handle most of the business, Daddy along with Mom and I moved to Georgia. Everything was going great. Daddy was only making a couple of trips a year to check the facilities. Then about two years ago, Daddy told me that my brother was stealing funds. Then Daddy changed his will, and it's now all mine. His beneficiary. When I started to see what was going on, I didn't want any of it. It's not me."

"Let's see if I get all this. About two years ago, your dad found out about the stealing. Last year, both your mom and dad died. You recently fired your attorney. Last night you were kidnapped. Doesn't all that seem a little fishy?"

"No. Yes. Maybe. I don't know. Does it?"

"How did your mom and dad die?"

"Auto accident. A drunk driver hit them."

"Guess there was a trial, right? What happened to the drunk driver?"

"Yes, there was a trial. The drunk, he got a year in jail, I think."

I promised her, "I'll get his name and look into his past."

"No need to look that up. I'll remember his name forever: George Kaplan."

"Interesting. I think I've heard that name before. I'll have one of my guys do a little digging. And don't worry, he nor anyone will know of the digging."

"Did I just give you a *lead*? Like Vivian gave to Bogart in *The Big Sleep*?"

"You sure did. I must admit, I'm very impressed. Okay, Miss Bright Eyes, who played Vivian?"

"Lauren Bacall," she said as she smiled. This time it was a happy smile.

"You just topped the list in my book. I have an idea. Give me your dad's name, your brother's name, and the attorney. I'd like to see if they had any connections, and if so, when. Too many things seem to be linked."

Nancy gave me the names and I passed them on to my guys in Atlanta. When there's money and power involved, it draws the crookedness out of some people.

"There it is. Lafayette has arrived. And there's a clothing store. Let's see what they have."

I parked as close as possible to the front door. I had kept watch and seen no one following us. There was little traffic, and nothing looked suspicious. It was to be a quick stop.

We needed a reason why she had no clothes, so I gave her my jacket to wear. With that she was only wearing the pajama nightie under my jacket and was, of course, barefooted. Once in the store, Nancy made up a story about us being on a hiking trip and how her big brother, me, lost her backpack in the river. That got a lot of laughs—at me. But it worked.

She picked two pair of undies, a blouse, a pair of shorts and long pants, shoes, and a few other incidentals. That was a start at being presentable, and we would get more. I paid for her clothes. It was then time for food.

I found a steak place, pulled into the restaurant, and parked. I opened the door for Nancy. It was polite, but it gave me another chance to look for anyone suspicious. I didn't expect to see any of her abductors nearby, but I had decided they had planned to kill her. I figured it could be her brother, who might be in cahoots with the lawyer. They would both benefit by her demise. I knew I had to get her home, or at least someplace safe and guardable. Her home might not be the best solution.

It was a late lunch and it went well. Nancy ate fast and cleaned her plate. I told her what I thought we must do. That she would be under my control till we could get her to a safe place, hopefully her home. She agreed.

She needed more clothes, so we left the restaurant and found a mall, where she bought several items. I didn't mind paying for them. We headed south.

One of my concerns was the vehicle we were in. A red Camaro could easily have been visible but not connected. I hoped. I doubt the bad guys knew of my car, but that wasn't for sure.

Traveling by air might be what the bad guys would expect. Driving during the day and motels at night would take three or four days, but could be the safest alternative. I'd have to convince Nancy of that.

Even through all that had happened, she seemed truthful, but there was also the possibility none of it was true and she had some unknown plan or scheme . . . for now. Traveling days with her could be pleasant or possibly fatal.

It was getting late, nearly nine o'clock, so I pulled into an upscale motel. While sitting in the car, I turned to Nancy to let her know of the sleeping arrangements. That item always needs to be clear.

"I'll get us separate rooms but close by, so if you need anything—"

"No way. I'll sleep in the same room as you. I don't want to be alone."

Decision made. One room, two beds, one bathroom. Nancy let me use the bathroom first to do my bedtime things. I texted my lead agent with the information I had so far. Nancy finished her bathroom tasks and was very noticeable when she came out. Yes, she had on pajamas. Make that a pajama top and very short bottoms. And yes, great legs. We each climbed into our respective beds. We were lying there on our sides facing each other, trying to decide who would talk first. Nancy took the initiative.

"David, you've been the sweetest and most considerate man I've known since my father. You've not tried to hurt me or take advantage of me. When I climbed into your car, I was more frightened than I could ever imagine. But that's gone. I feel so safe with you. And—and I'm wondering if you're wanting to be here with me in bed. Me, I'm thinking how nice that would be. But I can't. I just can't. Please understand?"

"The sleeping arrangements are just fine. I don't take advantage of women. My mother taught me well. Course, that may be why I'm twenty-six and not married. Maybe I don't take advantage of situations."

She was smiling a lovely smile. "Don't give up. You never know when that woman will show up."

"Looking at you reminded me of the saying 'The face that launched a thousand ships.' "

"That's sweet. You should be a poet."

"I get the feeling you never heard of the Trojan War and Helen of Troy?"

"No, I'm sorry, I haven't."

"May I tell you the story? It's a short one."

"Yes, please. I'd like to hear it."

"Here goes. Now, there are variations of this, depending on which philosopher you want to believe, and there were

Greek gods involved, so it gets sorta tricky, so we'll go with my version. Okay. The Greeks and Trojans were at war, and Helen and this prince or king or some great guy was her lover in Troy. Well, the Trojans managed to kidnap her, and her husband got very upset."

Nancy jumped in. "That had to be heartbreaking. How did he get her back?"

"Well, there's no historical record of how he did it. It was in a book. I forget the name, but I wish to believe he had his people build ships, maybe with help from the gods, and he got ships from his close friendly nations, and bingo, he had the largest fleet of ships ever. Then they sent the thousand ships to Troy and rescued her. My version would not stand up in any classroom, but Mom always said it's the thought that counts."

"I don't care what anyone says, true or untrue. I love your story. And it *is* the thought that counts. Thank you, David." She ended that with a soft goodnight.

I said goodnight and hoped she never passed that along to anyone. Paris would not appreciate it, and I could be in a lot of trouble with my college instructors. My current trouble was the next day, the long trip home, and getting her back to Georgia unharmed.

It was just past midnight when I was woken by a scream. I sat up and saw Nancy sitting up in the bed. No one else was in the room. She was crying.

I got out of bed and tried to calm her as I got on her bed and held her. Still trying to console her, I asked what happened. She said they were in the room. I didn't have to ask who, but told her it was a bad dream and that I was there to protect her. That she was safe. She was calming down, and I moved slightly to adjust myself. She grabbed my T-shirt. Still afraid. She wouldn't let go. I then understood how the next few days could be.

Decision time. I picked her up and put her in my bed. I lay down behind her and put my arms around her. "Listen. I won't let anything happen to you. Until you're sleeping better, you'll sleep with me. Just sleeping. Is that understood?"

She gave a quiet yes and slept the rest of the night.

That night told me the rest of the nights would or could be traumatic. I had roughly calculated it would be about a thirty-hour drive to Georgia. I figured with Nancy along, I'd be lucky to get eight or nine hours actual driving per day. I had three possible routes back. I decided to take the lower southern route down through Texas, missing Oklahoma but catching Dallas, Shreveport, and Jackson.

The Mississippi River might be a good diversion. It would be about three days and nights, assuming no unexpected confrontations. That was longer than I'd planned to be away. As secretly as possible, I'd been checking in to see if my family was okay.

We ate a full breakfast and left early.

We finished day one with another nine hours of drive time. With a little fast food, we had made it to Wichita Falls. We did stop several times to rest my eyes, hands, and feet, and to give me and Nancy time to get to know each other better. I found another decent hotel, and we began to get ready for bed. She was relaxing much better, and that night her sleep was more normal. We planned to head out early the next morning with a planned stop in Jackson to see the river. From there we'd head for Birmingham and park for the night. That would be the last night before home.

While Nancy was asleep or getting ready for bed, I continued to pass information to my agents, keeping it as private as possible. They were making good progress.

The same day Nancy had fired her attorney, Ben Cochran, he had begun to have phone calls with her brother, Frank. Lots of them. My agents, working close with the local police, kept the kidnapping quiet. They did a detailed search of Nancy's place, talked to neighbors, but didn't place any yellow crime-scene tape. They found a drop of blood on the bed. Nancy had no cuts that I'd seen.

I told my team the blood must belong to one of the kidnappers. That was a very good lead. And Kaplan, when his attorneys pulled some fast law move and got him released, he'd disappeared to the point he didn't seem to exist.

Day two started with an early breakfast. The day was going well, and Mississippi was amazing as always. Nancy hung close to me the whole time there. We weren't near the water, but it was so massive it could be intimidating. We passed through Shreveport on the way to Birmingham.

Nancy was talking all over the place, pointing at every tree or building or stream she saw. All was well till I got a call from Jennifer, my lead agent, at an inopportune time. Nancy was right there—listening. I was on my Bluetooth. I had no choice and took the call.

"Hi, Jennifer. Sure. That's good. Now she's out of danger. I agree. Yeah. Is there a connection? Interesting. But we don't have enough to arrest them, do we? I see. Then get a court order. Oh, you have. That's great. At least we can check their communication. Tell the gang good job for me. They did what? Really. Well, I hope it works out that way. But I have a lot of explaining to do. I hope so too. Good, guess I best take my medicine. Call if anything new turns up. Will do."

Nancy was looking at me. No smile. I was falling in love with this woman. I hadn't lied to her, I just hadn't told her all I was.

She finally spoke. "You *are* going to tell me what's happening? Who were you talking to?"

"One of my agents. They found and have the two guys who abducted you. They're in custody, and we have linked your brother and the attorney to your kidnapping." She was silent. I couldn't tell if the look on her face was happiness or anger. She had almost no expression.

"David. Who are you?"

I asked her to wait till I stopped. I was condemning myself, so why not? I pulled off at the next exit and parked.

"Nancy, believe me, I have not lied to you, I just haven't told you everything. I'm an FBI agent. I manage a crime division in Atlanta. I was in Denver reporting on a case when we met. When you didn't want to go to the police, I didn't want to say anything. You were so afraid I didn't want to cause you more concern."

"I thought I could trust you. You kept things from me. Oh God, why was it you?"

Gesturing helplessly, I answered, "My concern for you grew to caring, then deeper. All I wanted to do was protect you and find the criminals so you could be safe forever. Yesterday when you took my hand as we walked by the river, I knew I was falling for you. Then you kissed me, and you had my heart. But I couldn't figure out how to tell you who I really am. I wanted to, but was afraid what you would do. I am so sorry."

My words made no difference. She looked at me with an awful look. "Take me home."

It was eight and we were near Birmingham. If I kept driving, I'd have her home before daylight. I waited a few miles before adding, "There's more you should know. I said I was not married, which is true. But I was married. I married Amy seven years ago. She died of a disease that has no cure. That was nearly five years ago. I have two little girls. Patty is six. Linda is five." Nancy was now looking at me. "They stay with my mom when I travel. They're with her now."

Nancy's eyes began to tear up. "Had it not been for me, you would have flown back and been with them now."

"I'm often gone for a week. They're used to my travels. Please try to understand. After that first night when you woke up screaming, I didn't want to cause you any concern for me. By then I was more than just helping you. I personally care for you. More than care."

"David, I don't want to go home."

"Sure. I'll get a nice motel for you."

"No, David. I want to go home with you. Can I go home with you? Please?"

"I'd like that. We'll pick up the girls at Mom's."

"I forgot about them. Maybe I should go to my home."

"Why?"

"The girls. I don't want to hurt your family."

"The girls will love you. They need a female around. Mom's been after me to meet someone. Every time I work on a case, she asks me if there's a girl involved. And no more of that hotel talk. You're my girl now. My Helen of Troy to take home to safety. Right?"

She said yes in the most pleasing way.

I called Mom and told her I was coming to pick up the girls with my girlfriend. I gave the phone to Nancy as instructed by Mom. I swear they talked till we were nearly home. Okay, maybe not that long, but I'm almost certain they started with my birth.

With the evidence I brought with me and the data my team found, the pair, her brother and the attorney, was put away for a long time. The girls took an instant liking to Nancy. Mom did too, especially after the wedding. The girls really enjoyed helping Mama Nancy feed their new brother. To you guys out there, when a woman needs help, I suggest you help.

Oh, did I mention Nancy bought me a perfectly restored 1982 red Camaro with XM and GPS added? Things worked out for me, too.

THE END and a New Beginning

Out of Gas

Yesterday at 7:00 p.m., I got called to the Peachtree office and managed to leave at 2:00 a.m., only to get a call this morning at 6:00 to show up ASAP. Skipping breakfast, I headed out. But it didn't end. Halfway to the office they called to say they had found and fixed the problem. With little confidence the day would get any better, I did a U-turn and headed home. That was when she entered my world.

Ellis Road was about a mile back, and just ahead of me was a long-haired brunette in very short shorts walking on the side of the road. It was a four-lane and there was not much of an edge. As I passed her, the brief glimpse was breathtaking. Okay, you're thinking, *He just wants to pick her up*—and you're right, but also consider she could've been hurt.

With a quick pullover to the side, I stopped, put my red convertible Corvette in park, stepped over the driver's seat into the back seat, and to add flavor, rolled over the trunk with my feet ready to touch down—and looking really cool.

However, having slipped and landed on my derrière, my exhibition had flaws. Picture this: I was sitting on the grass, with small rocks for comfort, legs spread, watching Beautiful walk up to me. At least she was smiling.

She stopped a couple of feet from me, hands covering her mouth that must have been screaming with laughter.

Trying to make the best of the opportunity, I said, "Hi. Could I give you a lift? Anywhere?"

She burst out laughing. She could not stop. My beard must have grown six inches before the laughter moved to a sweet smile. She was smiling, so I figured that was my cue to stand, but instead she pointed her finger at me.

"Stay!" she commanded.

I stayed.

"Do you always," she leaned in, eyes focused dead on me, "pick up girls this way?"

"It's not my usual method. But if it works with you, these rocks I'm sitting on will make it worth it." This was not a pleasant position. The rocks were small but they hurt. "May I stand up?"

"Sure." She stood up straight but didn't take her eyes off me.

Carefully lifting myself off the rocks, I leaned back on my car, trying not to scare her. "Look. My attempt to look dashing didn't work, and well, it should be obvious I've had no practice. But there you were walking on the road, and frankly, it didn't seem a safe thing to do, and I really just wanted to help. Honest."

"That's a kind offer. You may be telling the truth, but I don't get into cars with guys I don't know. Thanks for the offer, but I'll keep walking."

Giving up was not on my list. "My name is Nick. Nick Harper. Will you at least let me know your first name?"

"Hm, is that short for something like Nicolas?"

"I'd prefer not to go into that, but if it will get me your name, it comes from an ancient Greek origin. No relation. It's on my driver's license, but I prefer just Nick. Please?"

"Nick it is, Nick," she said, smiling. "My name is Nicole, and I need to get to that service station. My car is out of gas, maybe. Goodbye."

She started walking around me, but I couldn't let that happen.

"Nicole. Wait! It's over a mile to that station. Here's a thought. The guy that runs that station is named Frankie. He's a longtime friend. The keys are in the ignition. Drive my car there. I'll tell Frankie that you're coming in my car and to help you do whatever you need done. And I'll stay planted right here. You'll ride with him or drive my car back here to do gas or fix whatever needs fixing. That will save you some time and keep you safe. And it's all on me."

The smile left her face. She didn't move. She was quiet. Then . . .

"Why? Why would you do this for me? This could all be a hoax. I could steal your car. Why would you do this for a total stranger?"

"Honestly, I just wanted to meet you. People have been killed, hit and run, on roads like this. I caught only a split second of you in passing and wanted to get you off the road. I doubt this is making any sense. I was called into the office last evening and have had only a few hours' sleep, and this is probably a crazy, dumb thing to do."

With that I walked to the front of the car, stopped, turned, and told her to drive to the garage and talk to Frankie. Then I started walking.

The next sound would have been heard in some past time as music to my ears. A very calm, gentle, feminine . . . no.

I turned to see her get into the driver's seat. She pointed down to the passenger's seat. Talk about fast; Scotty must have beamed me into it.

Cranking the car, she gave me a talking-to.

"You seem to be and probably are a kind, sweet, and crazy guy. Yes, you must be crazy. Me too, because I believe you, and this is the nicest thing anyone has ever done for me. But I'm doing the driving." She smiled that sweet smile again.

We got her gas, and with a lot of encouragement, I managed to get Frankie to vouch for me. Note he took too much pleasure doing that. We've known each other since first grade and are the best of friends. He was the athlete girls were scrambling after. He always gave me his leftovers. He did manage to slip in some otherwise-best-left-unknown past adventures of ours. Nicole didn't seem to mind.

With gas in her car, I followed her back to her apartment. Nicole got out of her car and stood there, it seemed, waiting for me to join her. I stopped at a respectable distance, trying not to invade her space but hoping she would invite me in. She took two steps toward me, invading *my* space. Things were looking up.

She took hold of both my hands.

"Nick, you are a nice, sweet, thoughtful guy, and I would invite you in but, there's some things going on, and . . ." She looked at the apartment, chewing her lip as if there were something unpleasant inside. "I wish I could, but I just can't."

Now, she hadn't told me go vanish forever, and she had invaded my space. Hey, what did I have to lose?

"Nicole, I don't know what's scaring you. Listen. Let me take you to dinner tonight. If you want to tell me more, I'll listen. If not, we can talk about the weather or I can tell you of my near misses with girls, or I can just sit and look at you. How about it?"

Another eternity of silence. The population of earth doubled. Multiple universes were created. Okay, okay, you get the point.

"Yes." The universe was at peace. "Pick me up here at six."

"Six it is. And I will not be late." With that I jumped in my Vette and headed out.

However, as I was leaving, she did not head for her apartment. She stood by her car till I was out of the apartment complex. Out of her sight.

My suspicious nature kicked in. She had been going somewhere when she had run out of gas. And with a fresh supply of gas, she hadn't continued there.

I pulled over between buildings to hide. It was not easy hiding a red Corvette. I stepped out and attached myself to the corner of a building, watching.

Suspicious nature rewarded.

In under a minute, she rolled out the complex and took a left. I waited till she was a good distance ahead and began to follow, attempting to stay behind other vehicles to keep my red *look at me follow you* vehicle out of sight.

She headed into town. Turned on Poplar Street. And to my surprise, she pulled into the police station, the one that was once a grammar school. There had to be a sensible reason. She was visiting her brother who was a murderer. Her boyfriend was a vampire. Her aunt robbed a bank.

I pulled in, parked, walked inside, and sat down.

She was nowhere in sight. I was there about ten minutes and she appeared with an older man wearing a suit and tie. They hugged. He went back to wherever.

She turned and saw me. She did not look happy but started walking toward me. As she got close I stood up. I looked at her eyes and saw the tears start. Without a word, she passed by me and out the door. When I caught up to her, she was standing by her car.

"Nicole, I owe you an apology for following you. But I was concerned. Something just didn't seem right. And, well, I just want to help, any way I can."

Without a word, she walked to my car and got in. I joined her. I let the top up for a little privacy. She offered no words, but her tears said a great deal. After a time, the words came.

"Last night someone broke into my apartment. My personal things were broken or cut. Everything was ruined."

"That's an awful thing, and I can see why you must be so scared. But I'm thankful you weren't hurt."

"Oh, no. I wasn't there. I had spent the night with my friend Patty."

"So you found it this morning when you got home?"

"Yes. When I saw everything all like it was, I left. I was going to see my father. That's when I ran out of gas and you saw me."

"I now see why you didn't go into your apartment when I left you there. Any idea who would do this? Was anything taken? Stolen?"

"I don't know if anything was stolen. When I saw it like that, I was so scared I was afraid to go into rooms. Nothing like this has ever happened to me before. I don't know what to do."

"Could this have been done by anyone you know?"

"Well, I was dating a guy, Mark, for a few weeks, when he began to question everything I did. He even stopped me from seeing anyone."

"You think he did it?"

"Yes. No. I'm not sure. He even started accusing me of things at work. I broke off the relationship a few days ago, and now someone has broken into my apartment."

"And you reported this to the police this morning?"

"Yes, my father is a police supervisor. You just saw him in the station. Nick, I filled up yesterday. I can't prove it, but I think he drained my gas tank. He would do that sort of thing."

"Nicole, what did your father say?"

"They're going over there now to look it over. Daddy said unless they left fingerprints or DNA, or someone saw him, it would take a long time, if ever, to figure it out. Oh, and they will question Mark. He will know I told them. That scares me. Once, he raised his hand and was about to hit me." She was shaking. I gently took her hand.

"The police will do all they can and may keep your apartment under watch. But they can only do that for so long or until he shows his hand. And they have their limits."

"It's okay. Dad said they would figure it out."

"I know he will. But I have an idea. Now, you don't know me. We met an hour ago. You have no reason to trust me. Just listen. Does your ex know where the friend you spent the night with lives? Patty?"

"No. At least, I don't think so."

"If he emptied the tank, he probably did it at Patty's apartment. Don't worry. We'll work around that. It's too dangerous for you to spend the night at her place, and certainly not at your place. Here's the plan. You'll stay at my sister Anna's home for a few days till we see how this plays out."

Nicole started to speak. I told her to wait.

"You two are about the same size. Clotheswise that will work for tonight. We'll leave at six a.m. for your apartment, in your car, and get you some clothes and girl things. I'm thinking the bad guys will still be asleep. They tend to prowl at night. How am I doing so far?"

"I don't know what to say. I don't know what to do. Father told me to stay with Patty tonight. But maybe I shouldn't. But if Mark knows about Patty, she's in danger."

"I've already thought about that. I'll have couple of my guys watch Patty's place. You're going to give me Mark's address, and he'll be watched, too."

"What do you mean, '*guys*'? And everyone being watched? *Who* are you?"

"Okay. Confession time. My father was with the FBI for nearly thirty years till he retired. He wanted me to be an agent. He got me involved with all sorts of investigations. Most, I suspect, he should not have. He said I took to it like glue, but I didn't like the restrictions. Dad had a longtime friend who had his own investigation unit, Harry Kaplan. Harry was international. He was what was once called a private detective. Private investigator. A Sam Spade. Philip Marlowe."

She looked stunned. Puzzled. I added, "You have no idea who those guys are, do you?"

She was grinning. I had her distracted for at least a minute or two.

"Oh, but I do, Mr. Stone. You're talking Bogart, among others. And I'm impressed. So, you have teams working for you?"

"And I'm impressed. Yes. My main US offices are in California and Atlanta. Harry died three years ago, and in his will he turned everything over to me. He was my mentor. I think he knew his time was coming. When I look back, I see how he started turning so much over to me. He would be along, but he had me as primary on cases. He would direct questions to him to me. Before I knew it, I was working alone. I miss him."

"Sounds like a good man and good friend. So what are you doing here? In Griffin?"

"I'm here visiting my sister till I saw you."

"I'm glad you did." She was smiling again. "But where do you live?"

Somewhere in the talking I had let go of her hand. I picked it back up again.

"California. South of LA."

"Wow. I thought you were born in Griffin. The guy at the service station seemed to have known you for a long time."

"I was born in Griffin. Frankie knew me and still knows me. I didn't leave till Harry found me. Believe me, things changed. And we need to get things changed for you, too. As a start, I need to know who you told about the apartment."

"I called Patty and told her what the place looked like and that I was going to the police. I then called Amy and Emily and told them the same thing. No one else knows."

"When did you tell them?"

"At my apartment this morning. I called them when I found it."

"So they don't know about me?"

"No. They don't know about you."

"Let's keep it that way. The fewer who know what happened and what we plan to do, the better. Listen. We probably need to leave the police station before they charge us for parking or something. *But*, first I need to make some calls."

With that I called Atlanta and arranged for the surveillance teams. Nicole gave me Mark's contact info, and Patty's, too. Those teams would be in place in couple of hours. I called Sis and told her what I had planned and got her approval.

"Now, tell me about Mark. Where does he work?"

"He drives a truck for Georgia Highway Express."

"Let's go check it out. You drive."

I parked my car on the street. We drove her car to where Mark worked. We passed by the truck yard a couple of times, then parked inconspicuously and watched.

I started to say we could be there a while, when Nicole interrupted me.

"There he is. Over there. Dark hair. The tall one with muscular arms wearing blue jeans. Blue, striped shirt. See him?"

"Good description. Did you have to look to get that detail?"

"Sorry. Guess I was just going from memory. Thinking of the good times."

"Nothing to be sorry for. It happens. And I do see him. He's helping those guys load their trucks."

"That's him." She looked at me. "Thanks for understanding."

"Memories can jump in anytime, and often unexpectedly. You'll get no complaints from me. The good point is he's there and *not* following us. We'll pick up my car and head to my sister's home."

We arrived at Sis's house at 10:00 a.m. and introduced Nicole. They seemed to hit it off well. And being outnumbered, I followed any orders given. They fed me breakfast. Nicole gave Sis a rundown of the day, and they both had a nice laugh at my groundbreaking meeting with Nicole. The girls talked about themselves, each other, and about me. I gave the girls a brief rundown on some of my latest cases. Okay, boring, but they asked.

It wasn't long before Nicole's dad called her. When she finished, she gave us a rundown.

"Mark said he didn't do it and didn't know about it till they questioned him. And he had a witness who corroborated his alibi."

That was an interesting twist to the story. "Did your dad say who the collaborator was?"

"He knows but couldn't tell me just yet, that he needed to verify it. And Dad said I can go to get some clothes. Oh, they dusted for prints all over the house, and told me not to touch any more than necessary."

"That's good to know," I said. "They want to preserve the crime scene as best as possible."

"That's exactly what he said. You're really smart."

Sis took over that comment. "He better be. He's been doing it for years."

"Does everyone have to pick on me?"

Somehow I knew Sis would chime in. "Nickie, it's no fun unless we have someone to pick on. I was the youngest and enjoyed it the most."

Nicole smiled wide. "Nickie? Can I call you Nickie?"

"No."

Sis said, "Ignore him. Of course you can." She was enjoying this too much.

"Girls, come on. It's two against one and I got things to think about."

"Nicole, he sure does, and I think it's you."

"Really? Are you thinking about me, Nickie?"

"Yes, but not for long if you keep calling me that."

"It'll never happen, Nicole. Remember, he busted his butt to rescue you." They both started laughing on that one.

I gave up and leaned as far back in my chair as possible and closed my eyes, hoping my ears would also close. Then I felt someone lean on my chair. I opened my eyes.

Nicole was hovering over me, hands on both chair arms and a few inches from my face.

"I like you too," she said softly. "And I'll stop picking on you." With that she gave me a short peck of a kiss, then stood back up. I stayed put. Hey, a guy can hope for more.

Then she added, "Can I call my friends and tell them what's happening? They must be worried."

That brought me back to reality.

"Yeah, they must be, and I understand. But you have to be careful what you tell them."

"Then what can I say?"

Sis was watching and listening. Watching for me to put my proverbial foot in my real mouth.

I started, "Okay, you'll be telling a little white lie, but it's for their good and your good. Tell them you met this tall, great-looking rich guy and he promised to buy you dinner and—"

She put her hand up, stopping me right there. "Hm, am I describing you?"

"Sorta."

She leaned forward again and pushed me back in my chair, hands now on my shoulders. "I don't want to lie too much. These are my friends, remember?" I heard Sis snickering in the background.

As calmly as possible, I pleaded, "I give. Tell 'em you met someone and you're at his sister's house for a few days. If I'm the guy, tell them *Nick*, but nothing else. Don't give them any names or our plans."

"Thanks, Nickie." She gave me another tiny kiss. My reward, I guess.

She called the girls and gave them the skinned-down version.

I managed to survive that encounter. We did lunch, and Sis brought out a board game. We played a couple of hours.

It neared suppertime and the girls wanted to eat dinner out, but I wanted to stay as anonymous as possible. They conceded and ordered pizza.

As bedtime approached, they decided the sleeping arrangements. I got the couch.

We got to Nicole's apartment at 6:20 a.m. In her car. No unknown or strange cars were around. I went in first, and it was pitiful what had been done. I repeated her dad's instructions to not move or touch anything except as needed for clothes.

I took pictures. I was surprised her pictures and photos were torn in half but still somewhat in place. Looking almost untouched. With plastic gloves, I picked up a torn photo. Holding it under light, I could see prints in just the place to do the tear. I slipped the two halves in my shirt. Our secret. I then held my arms out for Nicole to pile clothes on them.

While loading up, I asked, "Is there anything among all this that you know for certain Mark touched?"

"He touched a lot of things, but I cleaned and washed everything to get rid of *him*." She paused. "That's not good, is it?"

"Even the pictures and picture frames?" Those were the most obvious that had been tampered with.

"All of them," she said, sounding like she was questioning what she'd done.

"Actually, it's good."

She clapped her hands. "Really? How?"

"Simple. If he did this, we'll find his prints, his new prints. That would be a lead. For that matter, any prints would be a lead. Course, I'd actually like to have his prints. I wish we had something he did touch. Your dad probably already has them, but not for me."

"Yeah. I see. No, I cleaned anything I thought he touched. Oh, wait. He changed a tire for me about two weeks ago, before we broke up. Does that help?"

"Very. I'll confiscate the jack and tire iron when we get back to Sis's house."

Gathering her items, we left. We had been there sixteen minutes. I had left the door cracked. I hadn't noticed any autos passing by, and no one was in their yards yet.

At Sis's apartment, Nicole hung up her clothes and changed into something less revealing. We left for my Atlanta office—notice that was a "we." I didn't mind. Besides, her lovely self was safer with me. We stopped for a late breakfast, then headed for Peachtree Street. I'll let you guess which one.

My guys checked the photo prints against the tire jack. No match. Nicole gave her prints, too. Had to be sure. No match. Whoever tore that picture was still a mystery. I sent a copy of the prints to a contact in the FBI. He said he should have a match in a day or two. Where was Abby Sciuto when you needed her?

I took Nicole for a tour of the office, which didn't take long. Some of my staff were out on assignment.

With that done, we stopped for lunch at Mary Mac's Tea Room. I wanted to impress her. On the way, I asked her to call her dad and see if they had made any progress. I asked her to ask how many different sets of prints they found. Six sets: Nicole's, Mark's, and four unknowns. After giving her another prompt, her dad said Mark's and three of the unknowns were limited to the kitchen, bathroom, and a few in the living room. One unknown was all over the place.

My feeling was that third unknown was the same as I had found. Her dad still had no info on the unknown prints but was checking. The race was on.

I ruled Mark out. He may have helped, but from all Nicole had told me, I didn't think he was smart enough to use gloves in her house . . . and neither was the unknown.

You're thinking the same thing I was thinking. The damage looked very personal. I had her call Mark and be kind and understanding. I wanted his reaction, and she got it. He pretty much told her where to go, that he was not interested in her, and that he had found someone new. When asked who, he only said his new girl knew Nicole and felt the same way.

Lunch at Mary Mac's was a special time. Nothing about her apartment, but it was on her mind, and so were her boyfriends.

"Those are real nice people you work with. They were very understanding."

"That they are. They've seen so many abnormal things happening to people, they seem to understand. And don't you worry, between your dad and I, we'll figure this out. And we'll make sure no one hurts you."

"I probably caused all this. When I was fifteen, my dad told me I was a bum magnet. He wasn't being mean, just looking at who I dated. Nick, am I a bum magnet?"

"You didn't cause this, and you are not a bum magnet. You are a kind, sweet, and very beautiful woman. Granted, you are a magnet—the kind that every man on earth wants to be near. Unfortunately, some are bums."

"Thank you. That's nice to hear. You're not . . . I mean, you know? You're too sweet."

"I've been called many names, but never that. The girls at all my locations are always trying to hook me up with someone. Hope that helps my cause."

"I'm glad they haven't had any success."

I must admit, the dessert had no flavor compared to the view sitting across from me.

We finished lunch and while driving back to Griffin, I wanted to know more of her friends.

"Nicole, tell me about your girlfriends. Who likes who best? Time spent together? Their beaus? Do they work? How long have you known them?"

"Let's see. Patty is my best friend. I've known her since grammar school. We share more personal stuff together than with the others. She has a very nice boyfriend. They've been dating for over a year. Emily had a boyfriend, but they broke up a month or so ago. Amy has a boyfriend, been dating five or six months. Also a nice guy. We double- and triple-date a lot."

"Did they come to your apartment much?"

"Patty did. Amy and Emily sometimes do, but not so much. We usually meet at Patty's place because her apartment is much closer to Amy and Emily. Like a central place. Also, hers is a bigger apartment than mine. Doing sleepovers is a lot of fun."

"We need to rule them out. Do you have anything on you or at your apartment that you did not clean that the girls might have touched?"

With her answer, we went back to her apartment.

Nicole walked into her apartment and stopped just inside.

"You afraid?"

"Yes, but more afraid of what we might find."

"Listen. That's very natural. And now is the time to think positive in favor of your friends."

She looked at me with a small smile and started looking. I told her not to touch anything that might have prints on it. I would do the touching.

Suddenly, into the kitchen she went. Item one: Amy liked coffee and always made some when there. The coffee maker would sit in the cupboard till she came back. Item two: Patty had left her a spare waffle maker. She loved to make waffles. Nicole remembered they all loved cookies, so we gathered a couple of likely cookie boxes and a canister where some were kept. We had item three. I placed the items in a box I'd brought with me.

I might mention this was done without disturbing any prints. Or adding any. I called to warn my office we were on our way.

All the guys and gals in the office had really gotten into this case. They all knew there hadn't been a woman in my life for many years and had their hopes up. That's what one of the guys told me in strictest confidence, in the men's room.

They had already made preparations and had gloves in hand when we got there. Tests were made and results found and fully documented. A good point to make here is that I had noticed prints had already been taken. The Griffin team was already in the groove.

We returned to Nicole's apartment and placed all the items as we had found them. We left her apartment, and she called her dad to tell him about her girlfriends and possible prints to consider. I suspect he already knew about the girls. Still, we would wait for his results to see if his matched ours.

No sooner than we got back to my sister's home, her dad called. He had cleared the girls and had the name of the bad guy, Alex Chandler, one of Nicole's ex-boyfriends. Alex was, shall we say, upset that Nicole had dumped him for Mark, then dumped Mark. Guess it affected his standing in the community.

She was shocked. I was disappointed. My FBI guy hadn't called me first. But I had more important business to handle—Nicole. I pulled her to one side.

"Nicole, you've known me for less than two days. When I first saw you, I was only thinking of a date with a beautiful woman. But being with you the better part of the time changed things. I no longer want a date. I want a lifetime companion. You're twenty, and I'm nine years older. I'm not much to look at, and you know I'll travel a lot, and you know you'll have to move to California, and you know—" She put her fingers to my lips and shushed me.

"When I was five years old, my father was showing me old movies from the thirties, forties, and fifties, and silent ones, too. I remember one in particular with Rita Hayworth and, oh, that dancer, Fred something, and a movie where he went up to her window riding a white horse, wearing a metal suit, and carrying a sword. He was coming to her rescue."

I started to say something, but she shushed me again.

"As I got older and did something bad, Mom would confine me to my room with no TV, no phone, only books. I read about other knights. Nick, you are my knight. You rode up in your marvelous red Corvette and rescued me. I was so scared and afraid. My world was closing in on me with nowhere to go."

Trying to speak, I was shushed again.

"Being with you calmed my world. You give me hope. I was protected. I am protected. You are my Grant. My Gable. My Bogart. I love you. Maybe it's not normal to say this these days, but I'll go anywhere. So long as it's with you. And it's time you kissed me."

I responded and obeyed her command.

Well that's the story. The ex-ex-boyfriend Alex was not happy with Nicole breaking up with him, and he had finally got the nerve to trash her apartment. As to a brighter side, he had not wanted to hurt her. He had only wanted to scare her, and had been successful at that. We were fortunate the FBI had a record on him. The Griffin police had good contacts in the FBI. Okay, make that faster-responding contacts. I must have a heart-to-heart talk to my guy.

Nicole accepted my marriage proposal. We've been together for over two years now. She hasn't regretted moving to LA. Her father has come to visit, and she has been to visit him. Her girlfriends have been more times than I can count. I've been outnumbered so many times

I've enjoyed it. I added some personnel to both east and west offices, allowing me to travel a little less.

Well, I must leave you with your thoughts. Nicole's calling. It's my time to change the baby's diaper.

THE END of One Story and the Beginning of Another

River Assignment

Paddling down Flint River, Harry wondered why he had volunteered for the assignment. The heat was unbearable. The river had to be dropping inches per hour with the boiling sun burning holes in the sky. The only positive thus far was he was going downstream with the current doing all the work.

All he had been told was to go down the river till the first turn, then park the boat. The rest of his detailed assignment would be on the left bank.

The curve finally made itself visible a few hundred feet ahead. He guided his boat to the left side, parked it on the bank, and started looking for something. Would he find a shovel and an X on the ground and dig? Just as the shovel idea began to leak from his brain, he spotted a green envelope pinned to a tree.

Harry opened the envelope, finding a single sheet of paper stating:

Continue on down river. Pull ashore again at the next curve. Make little noise. Three hundred feet downstream there is a wood shack. There is a woman and her five-year-old child being held captive. Our informant told us there would be at least three men in the shack. Could be one more, but that has not been confirmed. We can't tell you what the woman and young girl are being held for at this time. They must be freed and brought back to headquarters. Do whatever is necessary to free them. Destroy these instructions.

His first thought was, *Why destroy the instructions?* Some idiot had left them out in plain sight, and the kidnappers may have already been expecting him. He planned to discuss this with his superiors, assuming he got out of this alive.

He executed the first step and headed downstream to find the cabin. He had to assume the cabin was near the river, if only for ease of travel. He pulled ashore at the assigned curve and headed inland about two hundred feet, then turned south watching his surroundings, as there could be someone watching him. It wasn't long before he saw smoke.

Moving slowly and silently, he could see the cabin near the river. It appeared to be about sixty or seventy feet from the water's edge. There were two rowboats, each with an engine pulled up on the shore. They did not appear to be anchored to anything on shore. From his position, he could see a rear door and a rear window, and one window on the side of the cabin.

There was light in the cabin but no visible movement.

Harry backed up several feet and shifted toward the river for a better view of the cabin front. He could now see the front door and at least one front window.

Remaining low, he maneuvered back a hundred feet or so to determine his next move. He needed a diversion, something to draw some of the bad guys out of the cabin.

Returning to his boat upstream, Harry knew the diversion had to appear normal for the river. Nearby he saw a dead but unbroken log.

He stashed his shirt, shoes, and his Austrian Glock 17 for his return. He knew the 17 would be more than adequate for the close encounters he would soon experience. He then positioned the log at the shoreline and slipped into the river. Guiding it carefully, he got to a position maybe a hundred feet from the boats.

Watching the currents, he gave his log a heavy push. The log was heading straight for the boats, but it hit something under the water that pushed it out, missing the boats by a few feet.

Harry remained as submerged as he could while watching the cabin. No one came out, meaning no one saw the log or even cared. He continued to wait for ten minutes, then made his way back up to his safe place. There was no choice. He had to try again.

He found another log, bigger than the first one. He knew he would have to guide the log closer to be sure it remained on target.

Preparing himself again, he began to guide the log downstream. He was watching for the spot where the first one had deviated from its route. The underwater item that had crashed his first try was a large stump.

He held on to the log as the current dragged him over that stump. Scratched but still on target, he was within sight. He maneuvered the log and gave it a heavy push. He then pushed himself back upstream and out of the water to get to his clothes and, most importantly, the Glock. He checked his pants pocket for the extra clips.

As he climbed ashore, he heard the crash of the log hitting the boats. He saw both boats quickly pushed into the river current and rapidly moving downstream. All was good so far.

Two men rushed out of the house. As they saw the boats disappearing downstream, they ran to rescue them. A third older man stopped at the cabin door, watched for a time, and went back in. An additional light came on. Harry could see the man walking around.

Step one was in play. Step two had to start.

Harry retrieved and adorned his clothes and weapon and headed for the cabin's back door. With a quick look through the back window, he saw the woman, the little girl, and the only remaining man. This had to be quick, as the other two would eventually catch their boats. And they would have their weapons. That was a given. Harry did not have a silencer. Now was the time.

Harry found a handy, slightly heavy rock. The cabin only had one room, so he figured the rock would make it over and cause another distraction.

He threw the rock and, with a running start, crashed through the door. The bad guy was pulling his gun from behind his back and had it almost at point when Harry put two in his chest. One down, two to go.

Had they heard the shots? Oh, yes. Through the window, he saw them heading for the cabin. He had little time. Harry hurried the woman and the child out the front door, telling them to huddle and to tell the two men that the old guy had tried to shoot them and she had hit him with a chair. He had his doubts that would work, but there was no time. The woman had no gun. The two had to know there was someone else. He figured the two would split up, one inside, one outside.

He headed out the back door and waited at the corner of the house. Then he heard Man One running down beside the house. Harry stepped out from the corner and took a shot. One down. He stuck Man One's gun in his back pocket. The cabin was quiet. Where was Man Two?

Then Harry heard the woman shout, "Back now." It was show time.

Harry was two steps from the back corner. He swung round the corner, rolling to the ground, and fired as Man Two came out the back door. Man Two went down. He pushed the gun away from Man Two and checked him. Very dead.

With the coast clear, Harry went to the cabin and thanked the woman. He tried to comfort her and the little girl. They were both crying. He helped them back inside, but there was no hurry. The deed was done. After a time, he had them collect whatever personal things they had while he went after the bad guys' boats now sitting calmly on shore.

The day ended well. Harry headed upriver with his two passengers, but they continued to huddle close with hands shivering. Seeing that, he calmly reassured them they were now safe and that he would get them home soon. The little girl went to Harry and sat close to him, holding his arm. After a time, they settled and shared their feelings with him. The mother moved closer to him. The three talked about many things, the daughter never leaving Harry's side. It was a pleasant ride, made more so as his boat now had a motor.

He'd been told of another mission that was most likely already assigned to him. From what little he knew of it, the only water to contend with would be a few small oases in the middle of the Sahara.

A Motored Ending

The Yellow Shed

Some people take much too long to die, some too soon and others too quick. Uncle Greeley, he was an example of taking a long time. He was an evil man, mean to his wife, and whipped his children more than needed, and his wife.

Too soon, well, that would be my daddy. I always thought he was so sweet, he'd never die, but someone in Vietnam didn't know him at all, so they killed him. Then it was my baby brother, Jamie.

It was the hottest Mississippi summer we'd had in years. Everybody was going swimming in anything bigger than a water puddle. Jamie was no different, except there was some bug or bacteria, they called it, in that old, abandoned pool half filled with rainwater and who knows what. The doctors said it got in through his ear. But that didn't matter. Jamie was still dead. Everybody's life changed after that. Things ain't been the same since.

I don't get back to Adamsville very often. Matter of fact, I haven't been back to the house since I left, the year after Jamie died, except to bury Mama.

"My college studies kept me away" was the excuse I used. I know that was a stupid thing to do, but I did it. I'm a grown woman now, and I regret that. Daddy hadn't been long dead, then Jamie had died. When Mama's new boyfriend kept making passes at me, I'd had enough. I left that year. There were more reasons to leave than to stay.

Mama left me the house, and even with the sorrowful memories, I didn't have the heart to sell it. I hired a real-estate firm in the area to rent it and see to its upkeep. It was a small, simple house on the edge of town; that hadn't mattered when Daddy had bought it. It was "just our first house," he had said. There would be more.

My name is Maggie. I'm thirty-one, with a successful career as an artist, and no family of my own. I figured it was time to go home.

I was standing in the front yard, trying to remember if the front porch had always been green, when I heard someone call from behind me.

"Maggie, is that you?"

I turned, and I swear it looked like Glenn Wells. I hadn't seen him in over ten years.

"Glenn Wells. Good to see you."

"You remembered."

"How could I forget?" Very true. How could I forget my first love and the only boy to ask me to the senior prom? I'd accepted, of course.

He moved to within a foot of me, his blue eyes glinting, smiling, and pulled me in close for a long hug. I didn't mind. He was the best-looking boy in high school, and if I didn't know better, he was Dorian Gray and had a portrait in his attic growing old.

When he unlatched himself, only a little, he winked with an inquisitive look on his sweet face. "I'd give you a kiss, but your husband might give me a wallop." Yes, he was fishing.

"You see a husband around here?"

"Well, no."

"Then what are you waiting for? Unless your wife would do the same."

"Looks like neither of us will get a walloping," he said, the corner of his mouth lifting, then planted the sweetest kiss I'd had in years. Talk about memories.

When he asked if I was staying long, I said maybe. I asked him how he happened to be at this house when I got here. He said he had a friend at the real-estate firm who'd told him I was coming. After a few "did I know" and "did you know" questions, out of the blue he asked if I'd like to have lunch after I looked at the house.

I said yes, but could we go now, because the growing lump in my throat would soon make it impossible to eat. Maybe it was my memories or hopes or wishful, girlish pride, but I believe his insides jumped when I said yes. We went to a restaurant called Peaches.

The place was light and lively with a big lunch crowd. The walls were dark wood, the windows stained glass. It looked expensive.

"I apologize for the crowd, but this is one of the few decent places to eat, lunch or dinner." Glenn's blue eyes sparkled.

"It's quite okay. I really don't mind the noise. Actually, it's very nice."

His smile was grateful. "I'm glad you like it. I own it and another one over in Carson City. And if you look right over there," he pointed to my left, "you'll see one of your paintings. I have another at my home."

Guess some things do change. Daddy would have been surprised, and I wanted Glenn to know.

"When you, we, were young, Daddy never thought you'd make anything of yourself. He wasn't wrong about much, but he sure missed it with you."

It was one of the nicest lunches I'd had in a long time. Afterward, Glenn excused himself to attend a meeting, but managed to swing a date with me for dinner.

I might need a sweet, friendly face to stare into after going through the house. That's where I went next.

The porch had never been green. Mama had always kept it white. The shutters had sometimes been green, some years brown, once yellow.

I think the hardware store had a special on yellow paint that year, because the storage shed out back was turned that same god-awful shade of yellow. I have no doubt that God likes yellow, he uses it a lot on sunsets and butterflies, but I feel certain he didn't approve of it for our shed.

That was proven by the fact it had burnt badly about eight months later. I don't recall why, but once Mama changed it back to brown, there were no more fires.

I'm not sure why, but I figured I'd find my room just as I had left it. Like in the movies when you go home after many years. But too many people had been in the house leaving their memories. The walls had changed color, there were different light fixtures, and even the carpet had changed. I knew all this because I had approved the expenses; still, a piece of me should have been somewhere, but there were only blank, foreign walls and rooms.

Next on my list was the once-yellow shed. The year it had burnt and before we had repainted it, Mama had buried a tin box in the shed. She had told me I couldn't ever dig it up till she was dead. That I'd know when. That was really what had brought me back. I couldn't bear to touch it when she died. It hadn't been the time.

The shed was now a tired, weathered, sagging sentinel guarding my time capsule. I brought along a small gardening shovel. The box wasn't supposed to be deep. It wasn't.

I don't know how long I stared at it, all rusted and scarred, sitting on the dark-brown earth. She had it taped up to keep it watertight. I removed the tape, popped the latch, and lifted the lid. Her efforts had been successful. The meager contents were intact.

On top was a picture of Daddy in his uniform. After carefully examining every fragment of the picture and running my fingertip over the jagged creases, I put it in my purse. Underneath was an envelope with my name on it. I opened it. It was in Mama's handwriting, dated two days before she died.

Dear Maggie,

It must be time, 'cause you are a-readin' this here letter. There are a few things you need to know. I don't feel so good, so this will be short.

First and most important, I love you. It would be difficult to decide who loved you most, me or your daddy. You were my first and my most cherished creation. That's not taking anything away from Jamie. He has his special place, too. Besides, Jamie worshipped the ground you walked on. You and I both know things changed after Jamie died, and we both know why.

You always said you left because my boyfriends made passes at you, and I know they did. That's why I had so many. The last one, Jed, was the best, but I never did want to marry him. Your father was enough.

The whole reason for this letter is to tell you it was not your fault. You didn't kill Jamie. Some damn bug God created killed him. I don't blame God or his bug for it. It was just Jamie's time. You always thought if you had been watching closer, he would have lived. I know Glenn was there, and you two were having your time together. His daddy was worthless, but I always liked Glenn. Sweet boy. Truth is, if you two had been swimming, you might be dead, too.

You blamed you. I never did. Your guilt cut off a lot of talks between us. You're smart and strong. If you haven't given up the guilt, do it now for me. If you have, tell me.

Love, Mama.

My eyes were so full of water, the letter was a blur.

It's amazing how much you can keep bottled up inside thinking it's a secret, only to find out it's not. *Yes, Mama, I'm over the guilt. That's what brought me back.*

I put the letter in my purse beside the picture, then dusted off the box and laid it in the seat beside me. It was getting late and I needed to get ready for my date with Glenn.

The knock on the door brought a smile to my face.

"You look great," he said as I opened the door.

"Thanks. You don't look so bad yourself. So, where're we going?"

"There's a small restaurant up in Waycross. Thought we'd go there."

"Tell me. What's Peaches like at night?"

"Well . . . it's quieter, darker—" he started, but I interrupted.

"Sounds great. Let's go there. Hear you know the owner. Maybe you can get us a good table."

I got my things and we started walking to his car. Glenn opened the door for me, but before I got in, he took my hand, his eyes ablaze with passion.

"Maggie. You should know . . . I still love you. I've never stopped. There, I've said it. Maybe I shouldn't have. Wow. Gee, I messed it up, didn't I?"

If I had met him a year ago, all he would have gotten was a handshake. I might tell him that one day. The fact that I was able to come home and dig up the box, maybe, just maybe, everything was now as it should have been. I'd have to leave that up to the future.

For now, I would enjoy the moment and see what happened. Mama might have been smarter than I thought.

I put my hand on his blushing cheek.

"No. Not at all. A girl always loves to hear those words. Besides, you've already told me in more ways than one. I'm not ready to say them to you, yet. But be patient. Besides, Mama always liked you. And that means a lot to me."

THE END, with a Possible Future

Mystery Encounter

With a gesture that almost cracked the thick glass of the counter, Robert slammed the bottle of perfume down. He could not believe he had correctly heard the beautiful salesgirl's low words. It just couldn't have been what he thought.

Such things weren't issued from elegant, young, auburn-haired beauties who possessed magical green eyes, full pouting lips, and no rings on their fingers.

"Excuse me, Comila," he said as he glanced at her name tag pinned to a snow-white blouse. "What was that you said?"

She leaned forward, grabbed his shirt, and pulled him to her, now only a few inches from Robert's reddening face.

"I said, 'That fragrance would taste good on any part of my body,' and my name is Carmela. Do you need glasses *and* a hearing aid?"

Yes, he had heard her correctly. He had been around many women, yet none had come on to him so boldly, but even when they had, it always embarrassed him. It never proved fatal, though, the being flustered and the face turning red, that is.

The scary part was he had heard those words before.

His composure restored, he said, "I don't need glasses. Your beauty needs nothing to enhance it. And as to the hearing, well, those words can be found in any man's dream. I just couldn't believe . . . I mean, you don't even know me. Why . . .?"

"Oh, but I *do* know you, Robert Bishop. I know a *lot* about you. My name is Carmela Stracore. Does that ring any bells?"

Robert repeated her name out loud, then to himself. Was she a past lover, only known for a night in some foreign country, where she had whispered those words? She was young enough, or was it old enough, to be either. There was no foreign accent, nor a Southern one. There was little accent that might place her in Nebraska or Iowa, but then he could speculate all day. He just couldn't place her.

"Look, I'm sorry, but I just don't—"

She didn't give him a chance to finish. "My father is Dr. Benjamin Stracore. Does that help?" By now she had taken a more comfortable stance behind the counter.

"*You're* Ben's daughter?" It all came back. Robert had met Dr. Stracore two years ago in Turkey. The doctor had helped the Kurds, who had escaped from Iraq.

Dr. Stracore had been accompanied by his wife, also a doctor, and his daughter, Tracy, twenty-two, the only daughter Robert had met. Robert, on the other hand, had been helping with weapon supplies and other acts the CIA would never make known nor own up to.

Robert would always remember Dr. Stracore. Robert had managed to get himself shot. The doctor had saved his life.

"Yes, his youngest," she said with pride. About that time an elderly woman came to the counter. Carmela offered the services of the other clerk and shuffled the woman away. Then Carmela looked back at Robert with a quizzical look. "Why so surprised?"

"Ben told me he had another daughter back in the States, but I . . . well, I just figured you were much . . ."

"Younger?"

"Well, yes?"

"I was twenty and finishing my undergraduate work."

"So, your dad mentioned me, huh?" Robert asked proudly.

"Yes, he did, but Tracy told me much more about you."

They say that which you fear the most will come back to haunt you. Tracy had uttered those words one night in their hotel in Turkey.

"I don't know what Tracy told you, but she . . . we . . . she . . ." Robert could single-handedly take on a bar full of linebackers, or carry his wounded partner through hell in Desert Storm, or smuggle the doctor and his family behind Iraqi forces and back, but when it came to women, he was still putty.

Robert's hands were on the counter. Carmela placed her hand on his. "It's okay. Tracy said you were a perfect gentleman, kind, funny, and very brave."

"She was a very special woman."

They made plans to meet after work. He was to go to her apartment and wait. She gave him a key.

Her apartment was not what he expected. It was large but not well furnished. There was little furniture, only a sofa and a small bar, well stocked, he checked. No TV. No clocks or stove to cook. He made himself comfortable on the sofa and waited.

Carmela appeared just before eleven. She made Robert a scotch on the rocks and poured herself a glass of a dark liquid.

It looked like wine to Robert. "Say, what's the drink you have?"

"It's an old family potion."

"I'd like to try some."

"No, dearest. It only works for me. I'm afraid it would prove fatal to you," she said.

That seemed strange to Robert—a potion that was fatal for a man but not a woman.

He was about to comment, when she smiled. "Robert, you are a very handsome man. Where I come from, the men are much thinner."

Robert was feeling good, pumped up. "Well, I work out almost every day." He liked talking about his physique. "One thing that puzzles me . . . we never met. How did you recognize me?

"Tracy described your dark, wavy hair, your blue-green eyes, right down to the little crescent-shaped scar over your left eye. That and a picture Daddy gave me made it easy. Did you know Tracy had a baby?"

The question came out of nowhere. Robert was startled. "No," he said, puzzled, half expecting who knows what.

"Yes, she did. She had your baby."

This was news to Robert. It couldn't be true. Tracy would have told him, so would her father. They had been through a lot together. They were at least friends, he thought.

"Are you sure?" he asked. "I didn't know—"

She didn't let him finish. "It's okay, Robert. It was planned."

"I'm sorry, planned?" was all he could say.

"Yes. You see, that's how we expand."

"Expand? I . . . don't understand."

"We developed a flaw in our DNA that makes it impossible to procreate with the males in our species. We need a mate with unflawed DNA. The offspring then also have unflawed DNA. When Daddy saved your life, he secretly did some tests. He discovered you were a perfect candidate for us, for Tracy, so she seduced you. She now has a perfect little boy. He will have your physical and Tracy's mental characteristics. He will grow strong and brave just like you, but quite a bit more intelligent. Daddy told me to find you and do the same. I won't explain how, but we have our ways. Now that I've found you, in about four months, I too shall have a boy like Tracy's."

Robert stood up. "Look, Carmela, or whoever you are. You're crazy. You're pulling my leg. I mean, Tracy was super. A baby? She would have told me. And four months? No. You're obviously some wacko, and I'm gonna leave you with your dreams."

Robert tried to turn and walk, but he couldn't. Carmela stood up and put her hand on his chest, pushing him back down. He couldn't move.

"Oh, no, lover. You must stay a while longer, till I'm through. Then, well, Daddy will be here in a few hours. He'll decide what to do with you."

With that, Carmela's arm began to flex and lengthen. Robert saw it stretch across the room to the light switch on the wall near the door, fifteen feet away—and turn off the light.

THE END for One, the Beginning for Another

Nonfiction

The Attic

Until I was eleven, we lived in a large, white frame house in the country. It even had tall, white columns lining the front porch. I lived there with my mother, my Aunt Jane, and my grandmother and grandfather. Grandma and Grandpa's room was the largest and used for gathering when company came. Above their bedroom was the attic.

One Christmas when I was about seven, Grandpa told me Mama had bought me an electric train and it was in the attic. He promised to keep watch as I went for a look. Four steps led up from their room to a door that opened with a small landing. I had to strain to reach the wooden latch and lift it. From the landing, the stairway turned to the left, where steps leading to the attic were enclosed by solid walls on both sides. It was dim, but at the top of the steps, I could see the train over against the east wall. I carefully opened the box, and there was this beautiful, red-and-chrome Santa Fe Diesel—a Marx, made of tin or aluminum, .027 gauge. I took it out and played with it, then tried to put it back just like I had found it. I did that several times before Christmas, whenever my Grandpa told me the coast was clear.

At Christmas I acted very surprised, naturally. I don't know if my mama ever knew. I had a feeling Grandma did.

I suppose you can tell my grandpa was special to me. His name was Elijah, but everybody called him Lige. He was tall and lanky, like the actor Jimmy Stewart, and had many careers. He was a deputy sheriff, a motorcycle police officer, and a textile-machine repairman; he also worked on trains and who knows what else. He worked on trains when he was young. That's when he first met Grandma.

He was under a train with another guy working when Grandma walked by. He saw her and told the man, "I'm gonna marry that girl." Well, he did, and they had a long life and ten children.

When I was five, I remember sitting with him on the front-porch steps and seeing an olive-drab airplane fly over. I can see that plane so vividly, even today. The sun flashed off the glass canopy covering the pilot. It flew fast and low, right over our heads. I was excited to be there with him while such an exciting thing happened. I believe it was the first airplane I had ever seen.

Grandpa was the first to tell me about boys and girls, sorta. I asked him once how to tell the difference between a boy dog and a girl dog. He said, "The boy dog has a . . ." Then he made a curling motion in the air with his finger. That's about as close as we ever got to the birds and the bees.

Now, there was a part of the attic that was very spooky. Once in the attic, the chimney was easily visible, rising through the attic floor from the room below. To the left and right of the chimney there were two half doors, starting below waist level. Once open, I could see into the unfinished rafters over my room and the rest of the house. It was always dark, with many spider webs moving from the cool draft of the open door. The webs glistened from the light coming through the openings. I never entered that area. I never even considered falling through the ceiling, but that was due to my age. So what kept me out of that rafter area? Grandpa always told me Aunt Soap Sally was in there and she would get me. That piece of information and its appearance was enough to keep me out.

If you wonder why my grandpa never came to the attic with me, he had come down with arthritis and rheumatism not long after the time I sat with him on the front porch. He was bedridden for the rest of his life, about ten years. I brought my trains and track and set it up beside his bed so he could watch me play. He was the man of the house and my male role model. Grandma took care of him that whole time, bathing him and cleaning up after him. He fed himself at first, but after a few years, Grandma had to hold the spoon.

Then the sad day came. One day at school, at age fifteen, I was called to the principal's office. One of my uncles came to pick me up. Grandpa had died.

Grandpa and Grandma were married over fifty years. There's very few alive today whom I can ask, but I believe in all those years together they were in love. And I've often thought that after love, there comes caring, and that is shown by the sacrifices Grandma made to nurse her man. The caring makes the loving obvious.

To this day, one mystery remains. What let him know Grandma was the "right" girl for him? We'll never know the answer to that. But there is a greater mystery to ponder.

What was my grandma, a young girl, doing walking around in a train yard? A dirty, oily train yard. Maybe, just maybe, she was picking *him* out instead.

THE END

Sandy

It was 1946, I was four, and I got a puppy. She was small and had medium-length sandy-colored hair, so I named her Sandy. She was no thoroughbred, just one puppy from a small litter of my uncle's hunting dogs. She was medium height, maybe eighteen inches, part spitz and part chow. She may have had other parts, but I never cared.

We lived in the country, about ten miles from the nearest town. It couldn't have been more perfect. When Sandy got older, we explored the woods surrounding the house, we ran through the tall, brown rye grass in the pastures, and we splashed through the shallow branch we found deep in the woods behind the house. We explored everything and anything that interested us. All that to say we grew up together.

There was a time I found that one should not get between me and her, for she became very protective. Once I was in our driveway and a car drove up. A man got out and he and I were face to face. Sandy quickly moved between us, looking at the man and growling. I called for Mom. But you should know, she never bit anyone.

She did scare some snakes away. I was too young to be afraid, and thinking back, maybe she knew that and something in her character told her I needed protecting. You might wonder which of us was the master and who was the pet.

There were no friends within walking distance. And except for family, there was hardly ever anyone around, so Sandy and I did most all our playing alone. When my cousins came on weekends and I played marbles in the front yard under the big acorn tree, Sandy was there, watching. When I got home from school, Sandy was waiting for me. She was my best friend. When I got my first air rifle, we did some serious hunting out back in the woods. I never killed anything. I shot at a squirrel once. The BB hit him on his back and bounced off. He looked back at me, paused, then scampered on up the tree.

My family didn't let pets in the house except when it was extremely cold or very, very bad weather. A dog in the house just didn't happen, but I compensated. I built lean-tos and other huts where Sandy and I could rest from our exploring.

All that time I never realized the danger that ran along the front of our home. The house was up on a hill, the highway below. One day my world nearly ended. I can see myself now, standing on the hill, looking down. I saw Sandy crossing the road. She'd been doing some exploring of her own. As she entered the road, a car suddenly came around the curve. I screamed at the car to stop and at Sandy to run. She saw the danger, tried to turn. The car swerved, but the rear wheel caught her back leg. The force sent her spinning. I didn't think she'd ever stop.

As I started to her, the car pulled to the side of the road. The man got out of the car and picked her up. She was bleeding real bad. He apologized several times as he carried Sandy up the hill to my house. My grandma helped me make her a comfortable bed in the well house despite my pleading to keep her inside. Remember, animals were kept outside, but never mind, I would stay with her. My folks didn't call a vet. We were ten miles from the nearest town, and I don't know if it even had a vet in those days. And we were poor, so I guess it all fit. Grandma cleaned Sandy's wounds and made a bandage for her leg. It was mangled awful.

Except for the time I was in school, I stayed with Sandy, fed her, changed her bedcovers, and tried to console her as best I knew how. I couldn't stay at night, but the next morning I was out early to check on her. Her get-well time was only three or four weeks, but it seemed like forever. But Sandy recovered perfectly and we resumed our exploring.

We eventually moved to the city, and Sandy and I had a fresh supply of places to explore. There was even a small patch of woods out back. She continued to run and play, but by this time Sandy was twelve years old and began to limp if she ran and jumped too long and hard. I didn't understand it then, but I believe Sandy had arthritis, maybe from the accident.

Once again, the street proved a danger. One Saturday afternoon, a car hit her as she crossed it. The driver didn't stop this time, and Sandy was hurt very bad. Her right leg was almost completely torn off by the impact. The vet told us there wasn't much he could do for her, so he cleaned the wound and applied some bandages. She lasted three days.

Sandy died during the night. Death for humans often comes at night. Maybe it's the most peaceful time for death to visit.

I buried Sandy in the woods out back. We spent a lot of time in woods; she seemed to enjoy it there. I've had several dogs and cats since, but Sandy was my first dog and the one I remember most. I think you know what I mean.

When Sandy died, I didn't really understand how things worked, that in life we humans move from pet to pet, loving each one, always knowing we will lose them. She was a special friend, my first real friend. She never deserted me and was always there for me. You don't get many friends like that. Love and miss you, Sandy.

THE END

Through the Pasture

Every family has special people, and mine is no exception. I really know very little about my Aunt Mattie Mae, as far as what she did as a child or what her dreams were, that sort of thing. I do know this. She was a kind, unselfish woman to whom fate dealt a hard life.

She married a man who, for a time, drank more than he should. She churned milk by hand, drew water from an open well, cooked with a woodburning stove, kept her faith, and took care of her man through it all.

They were poor and lived what we would describe today as a simple life. Early in their marriage, before I was born, they lived in a small house on Georgia Highway 16 between Zetella and Senoia.

Now, here's the amazing story told to me by my Aunt Jane not long before she died. Aunt Mattie Mae wanted to see her mother, my grandmother, who lived in Griffin. Her husband dropped her off on his way to work. Her decision to visit her mother saved her life. A tornado swept over the fields and literally destroyed her home. Nothing remained but splinters and broken planks.

Everything was lost. If she had stayed home that day, I would never have known her.

After a time, my Aunt Jane and Uncle Brady bought one hundred acres of land near Zetella, on Georgia Highway 16. There were two houses on the land. Me, Aunt Jane, Mom, and my grandparents moved into one, and Aunt Mattie Mae and Uncle Brady moved into the other. Uncle Brady chose the smaller of the two, but it had ninety acres of land for cows and hogs. Their house was just down the road from us. Easy walking distance for a six-year-old boy—me. Their house had just two rooms: a kitchen and a bedroom, with the toilet out back, a two seater, next to the chicken coop. In the fifties they added two more rooms that doubled the size of their home, and added an indoor toilet. I spent most of my time in that little two-room house. As a little boy with my dog, I vividly remember walking past our barn into their pasture. I made that trip many times.

They raised much of their own food. They had a garden, lots of chickens, one or two hogs, and at least one cow. Now, my Aunt Mattie Mae was a tender person, but sometimes she had to do things that didn't seem so kind. When they had fried chicken, they didn't have a KFC to visit. No, they had to do it themselves. She would go pick a chicken from the pen and, I believe with as much kindness as possible, wring its neck. She then plucked two feathers, placed them on the ground in a crossed fashion, then laid the chicken on the feathers. She said the chicken would die quicker.

Uncle Brady raised most of the meat they ate. Once, he bought a small calf to raise, and yes, it was destined for food. Aunt Mattie Mae fed the calf every day, first with a bottle when it was young, then grain later. It was still a young calf when Uncle Brady killed and cut it up. My Aunt couldn't bring herself to eat any of the meat. She could still see it's big, lonely, brown eyes looking at her.

I once found two moonshine stills in the woods behind Uncle Brady's house. It's unknown if they were on "his" land. They were probably not his, but I always wondered. Generally, I think he was a good man. He did the best he knew in providing for them both. He was a barber and a farmer, and knew many ways to get things done. For instance, when Uncle Brady wanted his hens to lay more eggs, he put little Pond's cold-cream jars in their nests. They were white and must have looked like eggs to the chickens, because they would set on them and lay more eggs.

The first stove I remember seeing was a wood- or coal-burning stove in that two-room home, large, black, and with a smokestack going up through the ceiling. She did her cooking on that till he remodeled the house and she got a regular stove, along with a refrigerator that didn't need a block of ice to keep it cold.

A few years later, she got a washing machine. Aunt Mattie Mae had washed clothes by hand all her life until Uncle Brady bought her that washing machine. He enclosed the well, put in a pump, and put the machine in the well house—near the water supply, I guess. She would sit in the well house and watch the machine wash the clothes. I asked her once why she didn't do something else. I have thoughts of what she told me, but to this day I don't remember her answer. I think that keeps the memory sweeter.

And there were her biscuits. Aunt Mattie Mae made *the* best biscuits. They were about the width of the McDonald's biscuit we know today and about an inch tall, sloping down on all sides. Always perfect. She mixed them in a long, wooden mixing bowl, about three feet long, maybe a foot wide, shallow and oval. She kept her flour in a metal container in a white cabinet and would fill the container by lifting and pouring twenty-pound bags into it. I watched her mix many batches of biscuits; she always made a batch when I came down, and I could eat all I wanted, and would add butter and strawberry jelly. I know the butter was homemade. Bet the jelly was too. I can see them so clearly I can almost taste them.

Early on, they didn't have money to buy clothes. I know she made her own pillow cases and most of her dresses. She bought material, and with a pattern and a sewing machine, of the manual type, created the nicest dresses. Aunt Mattie Mae could tat, and the tables and shelves always had lacy, delicate, white dust covers on them. I still have some she gave me.

She always had an apron on, always with the same design. I believe she made her aprons from old flour sacks. There was a pattern, usually blue, at the top of those sacks. That same pattern was at the bottom of her aprons. This I do know. She made me short-sleeve shirts when I was little, and those shirts had a pattern on the shirt pocket, or around the back of the neck, or at the end of the shirt sleeve. It was that same blue pattern.

Being young I was sometimes a pest, especially in my earlier years of five and six. This happened when they were still in the two-room house. Aunt Mattie Mae had a small, decorative kerosene lamp. It was only seven or eight inches high, with a yellow glass globe, and a brass base and shade. I sat on the floor, and for hours would light it and blow it out, over and over. I have no idea what the attraction was, but Uncle Brady didn't seem to mind. He probably felt it best not to complain.

Aunt Mattie Mae and Uncle Brady never had any children. Not too long ago my Aunt Betty Jo told me a story that may be the reason. As you read this, keep in mind this took place in the 1920s. When Aunt Mattie Mae was young, she had gallstones and they were hurting bad. She went to the doctor and he cut her open. Seems he cut too deep and her insides got cut up too. She was bleeding real bad all inside. The doctor thought she was going to die, so he didn't sew her back up and left the room with her on the table. Did you get that? He left her on the table. Alone. Bleeding. After some time, he came back and found that she had not died, so he sewed her back up. Now keep in mind her insides had been cut up and bleeding. I believe this so-called doctor did not repair her insides properly, which could easily be the reason she never had children.

Following up on the above, she may have let me be her little boy. Her child. I visited her almost every day for eight or nine years—on weekends, after school during the week. I'd walk through the woods, then later ride my used bicycle down to her house. Never, never did she spank me. Never an angry word to me. I helped gather eggs from the chicken nests and sometimes broke one. She taught me how to milk a cow. I wasn't great at it, but she would let me carry the filled bucket back to the house. She taught me how to tat with a shuttle. I don't know if I was ever any trouble to her. Doubt I'd ever have known.

When I was about seventeen, I found out she had never driven a car. She had never been taught how. I asked if she would like to learn to drive. She said yes, but not to tell anyone. She didn't think Uncle Brady would've liked that. I found an old country road with little traffic and taught her to drive. It was a straight shift, but she did pretty good. She could finally drive, but she never did, best I know. Guess it was her little secret that I'm now exposing. She did so much for me; maybe I gave a tiny bit back.

When I was eighteen, Uncle Brady died. Aunt Mattie Mae told me he was out working in his garden, came to the porch, sat down, wiped his forehead, and died. She said it was just his time.

She went to live with one of her sisters, my Aunt Jane, after that. My Aunt Jane helped her sell her house and land. As I grew older, I visited Aunt Mattie Mae regularly, but not nearly as much as I should have. Guess that's just the way things are, but I regret not having been around her more.

Her final years were comfortable. After Uncle Brady died, she didn't have to work so hard anymore. I don't recall the cause of death, probably just old age. She was buried beside her husband in Oak Hill Cemetery in Griffin, Georgia. There were many at her funeral. She never had any children, but she had many sisters and they were close.

As I'm ending this story, memories of her pass through my mind. I can count the number of women in my life that I can name as a mother: my mother, my grandmother, my Aunt Jane, and Aunt Mattie Mae.

My eyes began to tear up as I wrote this. She cooked for me and mended my torn clothes, and I now wish and hope she looked at me as her son. I was too young to feel it then, but I feel it now.

THE END of an Era

About the Author

Winnfred Smith got his writing interest in Mississippi, where he met many authors as newsletter editor for the Mississippi Writers Association (MWA). Two things got Winnfred interested in writing. He was born in Griffin, Georgia, where in the tenth grade he took a typing class. He was one of two boys among twenty girl students. Ponder that influence. Then as the MWA editor, he met Eudora Welty, one of the many great authors of the South. Winnfred has been called a romantic, which you will experience in his stories as he blends mystery and romance.